Broken

DAWN

ANNA KATMORE

To Nicola.

Just because.

CHAPTER 1

Sebastian

"Titanium…"

FUCK!

"Sebastian," Noah moans, leaning against the bar in The Knockout while he waits for my kiss. The stomping beat of the club music vibrates through his body—as does the shock of Raffael's safeword through mine. When I brought the lanky student here after Raffael sent me away to find someone other than him to hang out with—something he'd made sure to repeat—I didn't intend to make out with Noah in front of him. Just a little flirting to show Raff that men could be together in public and not end up getting burned at the stake.

Now, as my lips hover above Noah's, I can't make myself move.

I've never wanted a guy as fucking bad as I want Raffael. The snowflake from Iceland gets under my skin every time we're in the same room. When he touched me so shyly yesterday after our videogame bargain, it almost drove me insane with the need to haul him closer and kiss him senseless.

So, why is this night in the club getting so terribly out of hand?

I don't usually set out to hurt people on purpose. But then I'm not used to getting wounded by them so deeply either. Of course, Raff didn't mean to inflict damage when he closed the doors on me. But he's afraid. *So* fucking scared of his feelings. Finding out after twenty-three years that you're attracted to guys more than women is a big bite to swallow for sure. But to pretend that it's not true won't get him anywhere but hell.

And I believe I just gave him his first real taste of that with Noah here.

I suck my lips between my teeth and blow out a

long breath before I glance at Raffael. His eyes are closed, and his throat twitches. His knuckles are white where he grips the Eristoff bottle in front of him, and his nostrils flare with every shaky breath.

Shit. I wondered for a while what his limits might be. I was so certain it would be a kiss, but I never thought it would be *me* kissing *someone else* that finally coaxed his safeword.

Tanja looks at the three of us as if she's watching an apocalypse. Which she is in some ways. Only it's the end of Raffael's life as he's known it for so long. Neither she nor their red-haired friend, Felix, can do anything to break Raff's hard fall. We're all frozen in place from the impact of his world shattering.

When Raffael opens his eyes again, his gaze is pinned on mine. His chest heaves twice, and his mouth is sealed shut.

"Raff—" I rasp, but he never gets to hear the second half of his name.

With both pain and self-loathing apparent in his expression, he smacks his palm on the car keys, sweeps them off the counter, and slides from the barstool. In a heartbeat, he's gone, pushing furiously through the crowd on the way out of the club.

Goddammit!

"Raffael!" Tanja shouts after him as she storms past me to chase her friend, Felix fast on her heels.

"Is everything okay?" Noah demands, his body tensing as he pulls himself out of his dreamy, passion-fueled haze and stares after the others.

My hand is still under his sweatshirt, but it slips away fast. "Listen, I should go after him and make sure he's okay. He's not used to drinking and shouldn't be driving his car tonight." Even though I doubt that quarter bottle of Eristoff Ice will affect his driving skills much.

"Yeah, sure," Noah says quickly, still seeming somewhat confused. "Take care of your friend. Raffael is a nice guy. I don't want anything to happen to him." He doesn't seem to notice what is really going on between Raff and me, but to heck with telling him what the problem is. Regardless, I'm deeply grateful for his understanding.

With a terse nod, I head off, wiggling through people as I make for the exit. Felix stands outside, and Tanja comes jogging back from around the corner, the heels of her boots clacking on the concrete. She smooths her snug gray tee over her stomach as she stops by us and, ignoring me, gives Felix a desperate look. "He drove off."

"Any idea where?" I demand? My car is just around the block, and he doesn't have that much of a head start.

Instead of answering my question, Tanja nails me with a scowl meant to annihilate. "Was that really necessary?"

Breaking through his walls and finally touching the very core that he tries to bury so desperately? "Yes." Since she's not really a great help right now, I pull out my phone and call Raffael. It rings a couple of times, then it goes to voicemail. "Fuck."

Felix, who seems strangely calm next to Tanja, tries to ring him, too, but drops his hand two seconds later and frowns at the display. "He turned it off."

"Where would he go in a moment like this?" I ask Felix, keeping my voice friendly but insistent. I don't intend to waste half an hour getting information out of the two of them.

He presses his lips together and then answers after a slow inhale and exhale. "Home. He needs comfort, things that are familiar."

"Felix!" Tanja blurts and takes an outraged step back, but he reaches for her hand and laces their fingers together, pulling her toward him again. She grinds her teeth, then tells him, "Fine. Then *you and I* will go there to see him."

"No, we won't," Felix says. The way he speaks with her, so tenderly yet with a tone that leaves no room for contradiction, makes me wonder how deep his feelings for her really go. And hers for him, when she blinks her dark doe eyes and pouts. Felix angles his head to me. "You going?"

I give him a determined nod, and Tanja grunts. "Why would you let him go after Raff, given what he did inside?"

"Because, much as I want to break his face for that, I think he cares. That's why he's here, looking like death. And...I trust him."

"You don't even *know* him," she murmurs with sulkily drawn eyebrows and puckered lips.

"Right. But Raff does." Felix pulls her into his

arms and strokes her back, saying much softer than before, "This isn't our fight, Tanja."

Wow. Raffael's friend just earned my respect. And Tanja, too, because she clearly cares for Raff. She loves him. I liked her for that exact reason the moment I first talked to her. And I understand why she's pissed at me now.

I take a step forward and gently grab her chin to make her look at me. "Hey. I'm sorry that Raff is suffering. I won't apologize for making him acknowledge what he feels, but I promise I'll go find him and make up for it."

With a sweet pout, she scowls at me for another moment and then sighs and nods, her chin still between my fingers. "Don't hurt him again."

That isn't something I can promise because I don't think we're out of the woods yet. But I at least say... "I'll do my best."

She takes the phone from my hand and punches in her number then hands it back. "Call us if something goes wrong, okay?"

"Will do." Glad she lost her death glare, I tuck my phone back into my pocket and head around the block to where my car is parked. The doors unlock with a flash of the headlights. Not wasting another second with even buckling myself in, I start the engine. It roars to life, then the tires screech as I give the car too much gas. It's almost midnight. There's next to no traffic at this time of night, and the drive to Mayfair is short. I try calling Raff again but only get voicemail, so I toss the phone on the passenger seat with my cap on top.

At his apartment building, I briefly consider parking outside, but I doubt he'll let me in if I ring the doorbell. So, I take the bend down into the underground car park and swiftly steer the Honda onto spot 37A. 37 is taken by the carbon gray Corvette. Thank God, he's home.

Once parked, I jump out and sprint for the elevator, where I impatiently press the button several times to call the damn thing down. Finally inside the metal and mirror stall, I punch in the code Raff used the last time we were here together—which I believe might be his birthday. It unlocks the ninth-floor button and takes me straight up to his apartment.

The entire ride up, my fingers cramp around the

metal bar behind my butt, and my gaze glues to the much too slowly changing numbers of the levels. As the door opens at last, dim light from the living area of Raffael's apartment welcomes me, but he's nowhere to be seen.

"Raff?" If he isn't down here, he must be upstairs, maybe in his bedroom or even taking a shower. Honestly, I don't give a shit which. I'm going to interrupt whatever he's doing. All I care about is seeing him and setting things straight after the disaster in the club.

Taking two steps at a time and gripping the handrail on one side, I dash up the stairs and then skitter to a surprised halt. Immediately, I realize that I won't find him in the bedroom *or* the bathroom. Because there's music coming from behind the other door on this level.

With my head angled in wonder, I slowly walk toward the playroom. Hand lifted to knock, I suddenly decide against it and cautiously open the door without announcing my presence.

Dubstep violin music welcomes me into a world that is as shattered as Raffael must feel. Looking around, cuffs, ropes, broken drawers, and a shocking selection of whips litter the floor. I hold my breath. The curtains have been ripped from the wall, the iron bar unhinged. The purple sheets from the mahogany four-poster bed lie tossed in a corner. The club chair that stood by the window has been used to destroy one of the exquisite shelves, causing splintered wood to scatter everywhere. Raffael sits on the floor in the middle of the mayhem. He leans against the bed frame, his legs drawn up, elbows propped on his knees, face buried in his hands. His white polo shirt lies discarded at his feet, and his naked chest rises and falls with his slow, deep breaths.

Reluctantly, I take a few steps into the room and, on the way, cast a brief glance at the display of the Hi-Fi system. *Underground* by Lindsey Stirling plays so loudly, Raffael hasn't noticed me yet. The sight of him so broken on the floor squeezes my heart in an unfamiliar, hard grip.

I consider squatting in front of him and cautiously stroking him out of his devastation. Maybe I owe him that—as an apology. But with all the rage in this room, it feels like the wrong thing to do. Raffael needs rules. He needs lines he can trace. Orders he can follow. There's a deep passion slumbering inside him that wants to break free, but he obviously doesn't know how to let it out.

Yesterday, Tanja suggested using the playroom as neutral territory. She was damn right.

My body tensing for a game that might take us both to our limits tonight, I stride toward Raff and grab his wrist, pulling his hand away from his face. I yank the shocked guy up to his feet.

Well, then... "Let's see if we can set this straight."

CHAPTER 2

Raffael

What the fuck?

I'm yanked to my feet so fast, the curse gets stuck in my throat.

Sebastian. The realization that he's in my apartment slams into me like a baseball bat to my gut. My lungs collapse, the air wheezing out of them. Shock widens my eyes as I stare into his determined face. He's in my room of rules and discipline—or what's left of it. I tore the place apart in a wild fury, venting all the hate and anger inside me. Most of all, I tried to shed the confusion, taking out my emotions on every shelf and item in this room. Now, it's a mess. Just as I am.

What the hell is he talking about? *Put this straight?* And how dare he enter my home without asking? My world... "You can't—"

"Oh, you bet I can." His voice is so cold, it's as if it's dipped in ice water. He drags me across the room and over to the wall. His grip on my wrist is like iron. I'm not usually a gentle person while in here, but Sebastian is clearly the stronger of us. "You feel safe when playing *master and submissive*?" he spits. "Very well, Raff. We're going to play a little now. Just you and me."

From the strength he uses on my forearm, I know his fingers will leave bruises before he disappears from my world again. "I'm done playing!" I snarl, fighting his hold. But he only catches my other arm and places both hands flat on the wall, reaching around from behind me.

"Done? You wish. We're just getting started, Iceland." His frigid laugh sounds next to my face. "What's your safeword again? Chicken?"

I tug my hands away, but he brings them back immediately, using more force than ever as he slams my palms against the wall. Feeling an undulating rage, I angle my head and glare at him over my shoulder. "Fuck you!"

"No." His laugh dies away, his gaze locking with mine. "Fuck *you* if you move your hands away from this wall even an inch before I'm done with you." His hard erection presses against my ass, and I know he's deadly serious.

I don't know why a part of me wants to do exactly as he says. Why there's this tiny voice in my mind, whispering that the forbidden will be so good if only I'd let it happen. But it doesn't shut up. So, when Sebastian takes his hands away from my wrists, I leave mine braced against the wall. The room pulsates with strains of electric violin, and my heart pounds in time.

He grabs a fistful of my hair and brutally yanks my head back, his body still flush to my spine, forcing me to look at the ceiling. I close my eyes. "You decide when you're ready to kiss me," he snarls in my ear. "But everything else..." His lips press to the side of my throat, his tongue swirling hard over my skin, making two intense circles. "...will be my decision from now on." And then, he bites.

Desire pools in my gut like the poison of a rattlesnake. Not long ago, I got the first real taste of Sebastian's games. They are dangerous. Merciless. And they always leave me splintered...a part of me wanting more.

His grip eases on my hair, and he moves his hands around my body, fiercely scratching his nails across my chest, leaving his mark. A groan escapes me through clenched teeth. Then he glides his flat palms down over my stomach to grip my hips tight. He slides the tips of his fingers beneath the waistband of my jeans and pulls me roughly against him. "Goddammit, Raffael," he rasps, "I almost wish you'd take your hands off the wall."

So he can fuck me? Yeah, I won't.

The feel of his fingers so close to my groin releases a tickling tremor inside of me. As he digs his digits deep into my flesh, I suck in a sharp breath, but the sound is covered by that of my fly being unzipped.

My erection grew the moment Sebastian named himself the master of the game tonight. Now, he releases my sex and strokes it, hard. His warm fingers wrapped around my cock make me whine. From shame...and pleasure. Every fucking nerve ending in my body prickles and comes alive. Jesus Christ!

Kissing the crook of my neck as my head rests on his shoulder, he murmurs against my skin. "Mmm...so hard..." His thumb whisks over the blunt head of my erection, wetting it before he begins a massage that weakens my knees. With my lips compressed into a harsh line, I puff out shallow, husky breaths through my nose.

"Do you even know how much your scent of snow and ice drives me crazy?" His purr turns into a hot, wet growl against my skin. "It has from the first moment I got close to you." He brings his teeth down on my shoulder, and a tiny cry breaks free from my throat. The twinge of his bite shoots straight down through my body and makes my cock twitch in his skilled hands. Bloody hell, there's such a thin line between pain and pleasure.

The rush of my blood in my ears drowns out the violins for seconds on end. Desire builds fast, and Sebastian notices, because his fingers suddenly slide away and move back over my body. They glide up until he grips my chin and jerks my head around so I'm forced to look into his eyes.

"I finally figured it out, snowflake. Why, in spite of all the rules you impose on yourself, you seek dares so much." His impassionate gaze is dark, lecherous. It bores deep into my eyes, and I feel as if he's setting my soul on fire with it. "It's your only escape from the cage you've locked yourself in. Your only chance to try all the things you would so love to do...with other men. With *me*." He runs his thumb across my bottom lip, dragging it hard to the side. "But you don't allow yourself any of that." Lifting my face, he kisses me under the chin and then nibbles a path down to my collarbone. "A dare is your excuse to break the rules. To push past your limits..." His words are a seductive purr. "Is it not?"

I wouldn't know.

His hands glide down my torso again, his lips still locked on my skin. "Am I right, Raff?"

Maybe.

I find thinking extremely difficult right now.

With his knee sliding between my legs, he forces

me to widen my stance. Then he shoves his hands over my hips, pushing my jeans a little farther down along with my boxers, freeing not only my hard-on but also my naked bottom. "Tell me if I'm right, Raffael." There's an impatient command to his growl now as his fingers dig deep into my buttocks.

For goodness's sake! "Yes!" The word tears from my throat, and I have no idea if it's the truth or just me giving in to the passion he ignites within me with every touch. Either way, I wish I could hold myself together and not shatter in his hands.

The breath of his chuckle dampens my skin. "I like it when we make progress." Behind me, I can feel him sinking to his knees, kissing a trail down my spine. When he moves his hand away from my butt, a sharp sting follows as he bites me hard. My muscles tense. "God, you're edible, snowflake."

I let my head fall forward, bracing my weight on my hands against the wall. Moments later, his lips glide around my hip to the front. One leg bent, the other stretched out on the floor, Sebastian sits in front of me, facing my erection at the precise position to—

FUCK! FUCK! FUCK!

His gaze captures mine, then he grips my cock and brings it to his mouth. His tongue swirls around the tip, licking up and spreading the arousal there. I pant, shock widening my eyes, sweat beading on my forehead and the nape of my neck. The heat sizzling through me desperately wants release. When Sebastian starts working my cock with his fingers in addition to his lips, I realize I might very well explode right in his mouth at any moment.

Leaving one hand on my erection, Sebastian pushes the other in a rough caress from the hollow of my right knee, up along the back of my thigh. Then, his fingers bite into the flesh of my ass. I suppress a yowl by sucking my bottom lip between my teeth and biting down, hard.

Sebastian sucks me in an enticing rhythm matching the music. It causes my cock to throb with painful desire, fighting for release. My toes curl in my shoes. His other hand slips from my dick and glides in a light caress over my balls, then around my waist to the back. There, his flat palm strokes upward over my ass, just once. On the way down, his middle finger dips leisurely between my butt cheeks. Holy shit! The asshole fondles my asshole.

Sweat trails from my hairline and over my brow, into my eyes. I blink, losing the tiny drop that falls and soaks into Sebastian's dark shirt.

I know why he's doing this. His gentle look still locked on mine explains that he wants to warm me up to the thought of someday having not just his finger in my ass but his cock. I want to close my eyes, block it all away. But he doesn't let me. His gaze holds me so tightly, it's impossible to break the connection.

I pant through parted lips.

Just a few more moments. Only a heartbeat...and I'll explode in his mouth. And the torture will be over.

Or...maybe not.

He slowly blinks his eyes and moves away from my erection. His breaths are unhurried and deep, his eyes trained on my face. What the hell? *Now,* he stops?

Licking his lips, he leans back against the wall. He's killing me with his silence. I don't know if I'm allowed to take my hands from the wall or not. And if I did, what would I do with them? Finish myself off? Fuck, I want to come. So damn bad. The tickle of pent-up lust at the very core of my body screams to burst free. Scrunching my face, my eyes shut tight for the first time in minutes, I let a low moan escape.

"Move."

The fierce command makes me snap my eyes open again. More sweat drips from my forehead. *What?*

"If you want to come...move." By the way Sebastian's eyebrows twitch just the tiniest bit as he speaks the words, I understand exactly what he wants me to do.

But I can't.

I can't.

I can't!

"You like to fuck to music," he says and manages to sound...soft. Gentle. "Then close your eyes and let the music take over." Leaving one hand on my butt crack, he gently wraps the other around my cock again. His thumb swipes the throbbing head, and he tugs—so close to his lips, but not quite there. His features are calm, yet his eyes bear a hopeful plea.

"Move your hips, Raffael."

I—can't!

His chest rises and falls with even breaths as he waits. He's giving me time, but he never releases me from the hold his gaze has on me.

I don't know what to do. I don't know what I *want!* A need builds inside me that eats up everything I've ever known, all I've been. It's as if it will bite its way right to the surface tonight, and there's nothing I can do to stop it. To keep whatever Sebastian started from happening.

"Move..." he mouths one last time.

And I do.

My chest constricts, cutting off my airflow as I slowly bring my hips forward. Sebastian guides my cock to his mouth again. His lips lock on the tip, and he starts sucking, letting me dictate the rhythm this time. I bend my elbows slightly so I can get closer. We look each other in the eyes. Every muscle in my body tightens. And then the dark strains of the violin fill my head as I fuck Sebastian's mouth.

In this moment, everything around me fades to oblivion. The room, the apartment, the building, the town with all the people in it. The rest of the world... Nothing matters anymore but this. There's only him and me. And the passion he unleashed inside me with the very first kiss he laid on my lips not long ago.

Nothing has ever felt so forbidden yet so good at the same time.

My world is unhinged.

And I don't know how I can ever put it to rights again.

Or if I even want to. Because Sebastian is the most dangerous dare I've ever agreed to. He makes me feel alive. Free of all the chains I'm usually tied to. He takes everything to the extreme. I never knew how much I longed for this—for someone like *him*—until this very moment.

I'm thrilled. And it feels like I'm falling with no safety net. No *safeword*. Just a jump from the sky into a world I never dared to enter before.

But with him there to catch me, it feels like a leap worth taking.

Slowly and steadily, I continue the gentle rocking of my hips. Sebastian gives me special treatment with his warm fingers and hot tongue, and I know that I won't last long. The pressure inside me surges to the surface, and a tiny twitch of my cock announces the moment that finally takes me over the edge.

Sebastian stares at me with something in his gaze that I can't name and swallows me whole as I lose myself. Letting my head fall back, a guttural groan escapes me as the waves of relief roll through my body, on and on until every last drop is spent.

My throat is bone-dry, and my lungs work hard to bring in air. I press my hands to the wall, grateful for the support now since I'm utterly unbalanced. As my head dips forward again, I instantly find Sebastian's calm and almost soft gaze on me. There's a little smile at the corners of his mouth.

With the hem of his t-shirt, he wipes his lips and chin and the spot on the collar of his button-down, before he gets up from the floor. As he moves away, I collapse against the wall, expelling a long breath. Then I turn around, drag my jeans over my ass, and zip up. My body is drenched in sweat, and I radiate a heat that frightens me a bit. But for once, I revel in it, as well.

Sebastian picks up one of the floggers that lie scattered across the floor of the room. With a smirk, he fixes me with his gaze over his shoulder. "Wanna play some more?"

I know he's teasing. Fuck, I *hope* he's teasing. But, not wanting to take any more risks or give in to his inclination to make reckless decisions on my behalf, I push away from the wall and stride to the door. "I'm taking a shower," I growl with an edge that makes it clear that we're done in here for tonight.

I don't care what he does next. Leave, head downstairs and grab something to drink, watch some TV until I'm done... It doesn't matter. He knows his way around my place, and I'm not going to throw him out. At least, not yet. But I really need to rinse the sweat off my body and, hopefully, clear my mind.

In my bedroom, I pick fresh clothes and then head to the bathroom where I drop them on the marble counter of the washbasin. I strip naked, leaving the jeans I wore on the floor, then walk behind the tall glass wall and turn on the warm spray.

It feels good to wash away the tension of the past few hours. Gradually, with the help of the hot water and some time away from Sebastian, my muscles ease, and my lungs begin to uncramp so breathing at least no longer hurts. I lather up my body and then drag my hands over my face, through my hair, expelling a deep groan of confusion.

At seven years old, I'd thought my life couldn't get any more complicated when I was forced to leave my home country and move to a land where people didn't even speak my language. Little did I know what would await me at twenty-three. This is so much harder than just learning to speak English without an accent.

Tilting my head back, I face the cascading water and sigh. Until a clicking sound makes me turn around.

The downside of living on your own is that you stop locking the bathroom door. And even with a stranger in your apartment, you forget.

Sebastian walks in as if we've shared bathrooms for ages, and this is the most natural thing in the world. Frozen under the spray, my heart leaps into my throat, and I pant through an open mouth. The shower flattens my drenched strands, and they fall over my eyes. Slowly, I lift my hand and brush them back, staring fathomlessly at Sebastian on the other side of the glass as his gaze roams down and up my body. I can almost feel it. After a slight appreciative smile, he heads to the basin, pulls off his shirt and t-shirt, and rinses the remnants of what happened earlier away from both.

The muscles on his back and shoulders ripple as his hands work the material. The mystical black Maori tattoos dance along his skin with every movement.

For a long while, I stand rigid, watching in fascinated horror as Sebastian once again intrudes on my world with absolute ease. His presence in the room crawls under my skin and numbs not only my tongue but also my mind.

When he's done cleaning his stained shirts and wrings them out in the sink, I long for the moment he'll leave so I can restart breathing regularly. Except he doesn't. He drapes the wet shirts over the edge of the sink and then opens the fly of his pants. After he pulls off his socks and tosses them to the floor, he pushes his jeans down with his boxer briefs, discarding them on a pile with his socks.

Seriously?

As he joins me in the shower stall and simply steps under the falling spray, shock grips me by the neck, and I retreat until the cold stone tiles behind me stop my escape. While my horrified gaze is trained on him, he doesn't spare me a look. What the freaking hell?

His body begins to glisten under the ceiling lights. I swallow, letting my gaze travel down to take him in. I've seen him naked before when he fucked Tanja, but tonight feels like a little show just for me. Firm chest, hard stomach, and a gorgeous ass. No one's here to share it with, even if the only thing I can do is stare.

With his eyes closed, Sebastian runs his hands over his wet hair, pushing it back. Then he tilts his head slightly in my direction. He looks at me again and gives me a small grin.

I cannot smile right now. I need all my concentration to keep breathing so I don't die. Because he's much too close. And way too naked.

While I seem eternally caught in my embarrassing

stupor, he takes my multi-purpose shower gel and washes his hair and body in under two minutes. Then he turns off the water. Stranded like a dolphin on the shore, I still have my hands on my stomach and chest, in the exact same places they landed when he entered the shower.

There's only one fresh, white towel on the shelf next to the shower. Sebastian grabs it and rubs himself dry, then tosses the used thing at my face, yanking me out of my stupor as I catch it at the last second before it lands in the wet stall. Reluctantly, I press the damp terrycloth to my body and begin to dry off, but my wary gaze stays glued to him the entire time. Holy cow, even just semi-erect, he's a sight. One that I really wish I could ignore because—

Ah, fuck it, who am I kidding? I've never been attracted to anyone like I am to Sebastian. Naked. Dressed. At work. Playing video games. It makes no difference. Even when he's just taking a sip from a goddamn Sprite, I find it hard to take my eyes off him.

The realization stings as much as the revelation that I want to touch him again. Wipe away the drops of water between his shoulder blades that he missed when he toweled off. They slide in an alluring trail down the valley of his muscles as he slips into his boxers and jeans. I can't look away.

"Can I borrow a hoodie from you?"

"Huh?" Startled out of my fascination, I lift my gaze back to his eyes that are now set hopefully on mine.

"To go home. I don't want to wear a wet shirt," he explains.

My mind still reeling from the events of this crazy night and the bizarre week in general, I nod.

He looks at me for another moment before he starts laughing. "Okay, never mind. I'll go find one myself." In a heartbeat, he's out of the bathroom. The sound of the door to the left clicking open drifts inside, and I'm left alone. I take the opportunity to finish rubbing my body and hair dry and then put on the jeans and white hockey tee I brought in with me earlier. As I step into the hallway moments later, Sebastian comes out of my room, looking down at his fingers as he zips up one of my dark blue hoodies, covering his naked chest. It has white words on the back, *JUST OVERTAKE. I LOVE TO HUNT!!!* and a picture of a mean-looking racecar over the heart on the front.

I stop dead. When he looks up, he does, too. Five feet separate us. We stare into each other's eyes, and his hands slowly drop from the zipper. There's a moment of tension that sizzles on my skin like a million ladybugs crawling over my flesh.

My gaze falls to his mouth. Earlier tonight, he said I'd be the one to decide when I was ready for a kiss. I swallow.

I'm not ready yet. I'm just *not*. But, hell, I can't stop looking at those lips.

With a slight frown, Sebastian tucks his hands into the pockets of his jeans and tilts his head a little. He's great at reading me. Even from the first day we met. He wouldn't have kissed me to begin with if he wasn't. Does he know how much every single cell in my body burns to taste the forbidden again? My heart rages in my ribcage, and I realize I'm unable to cope with the speed of my thoughts. I blink, but I'm still incapable of moving even one tiny inch.

In the next instant, Sebastian's curious expression

eases into a small, soft smile. He takes two strides forward, pulls one hand out of his pocket, grabs my neck, and presses his lips to my ear, coaxing out my shocked gasp. "Not tonight," he rasps. "Not when you're still so scared."

My throat and mouth are dry, my stomach roils, and my skin burns from the nape of my neck down. I cannot even react, other than to briefly close my eyes and let his words stoke my longing.

No...I'm just not ready yet.

He lets go of me and slides his fingers along the handrail as he heads down the winding staircase. Reluctantly, I step toward the edge of the landing, but then stop and just watch him go.

"By the way, Raff," he calls up to me as he lopes down the last stairs. He doesn't turn around. "Don't make plans for next weekend. We're going on a trip." He pauses, finally turning to shoot me a quick smirk over his shoulder as he heads across the living room to the door. "And we'll stay overnight."

Immobile, I remain at the top of the stairs, gripping the handrail for support. Then, he's gone, and the door falls shut.

My brows quirk in utter confusion, and I let out the breath I didn't realize I'd been holding.

CHAPTER 3

Raffael

With my mind still on the night's roller coaster ride, I fall asleep late and sleep long into the day. A strange sound like a table being moved somewhere outside my bedroom finally drags me out of my restless dreams.

I rub my brow and haul myself out of bed. Quickly, I slip on jeans and then hunt for the source of the noise. It's coming from the playroom, and the door stands ajar. With two fingers, I push it farther open and warily peek inside.

The bed is made, the floor is clean, and all the drawers are back in their rightful places—the ones that aren't broken, that is. The heavy club chair stands by the wall again, too. That must have been the scraping noise that woke me up.

Quietly, I lean around the door and spot my housemaid. Her thick, steel-gray braid hangs over the white blouse she wears that hugs her stocky figure. She hums as she puts away the last handful of cuffs she picked up.

Shit, what time is it?

I rake a hand through my hair and step into the room. Guilt colors my voice as I croak, "You didn't need to tidy up in here. I'd have done it—"

She turns around and casts me a smile, the expression reaching her warm, charcoal eyes. "Good morning, Raffael."

I've always liked the way she says my name with her Spanish accent. She grabs my white polo shirt that she laid on a shelf and comes forward. Her hand shapes to my cheek for a greeting. "It's okay. It's my job." Then her face scrunches a little. "But I'll need your help with the drapes."

Sheepishly, I glance at the far wall where the bar still hangs unhinged, and one curtain lies neatly folded on the chair.

Her hand slips away as I nod, and I lean down to kiss the kind woman from the East End on the cheek. "Hi, Rosa." Since I moved into this apartment and wooed her away from the previous resident, she's become sort of a surrogate grandma to me, especially once my parents moved back to Iceland. Sometimes, I think she's the only reason this luxurious place is even a little bit homey. She and her delicious cherry pie, which she often brings me when she makes some for her family.

With my shirt in her hand, she walks past me and out of the room. "Is Tanja all right?" her concerned question lingers in the air.

"Sure. Why wouldn't—?" I break off and bite the inside of my cheek. "She wasn't here yesterday...when this happened."

Rosa knows my two best friends and is aware of the kind of extraordinary relationship I have with Tanja. She loves my friends as she loves me. Like we're family... Of course, she'd worry about Tanja.

Rosa disappears into the bathroom for a moment, her voice drifting out. "Who was here, then?"

Back in the hallway, a spicy, warm scent which I hadn't noticed before draws my gaze to the stairs. "No one. I was alone." At the time.

"Oh, good." Her words are filled with a breath of relief. When she comes out of the bathroom again with two more items of clothing in her hands, her gaze fixes on the label of the damp, dark blue shirt. "Did you try to shrink them with hot water?"

"Huh?" The single word escapes me on a rasp as a flood of memories rushes over me. A bite on my ass...lips on my body. A shower.

"This isn't your size." Rosa's voice hauls me back to the present.

"Oh, yeah," I stammer. "Um. They aren't mine."

Her gaze moves up to my face. I swallow. If she asks more questions, I don't know what I'll say. But she doesn't. Instead, she sends me her warm, grandmotherly smile and rolls everything into a tight bundle, presumably to take to the washing machine. "Are you hungry, dear? I made lasagna."

I love Rosa...for so many reasons. One of them is her homemade food. Another is her non-judgmental acceptance of my lifestyle. The urge to hug her and say "*thank you*" overtakes me, but I keep it in check and follow her downstairs. While she carries the clothes to the utility room, I take out two plates from the cupboard and set the table for us. She doesn't cook for me every time she comes to clean, but when she does, it's always nice to eat with her.

*

Later that afternoon, once more alone, I go on a hunt for my cell phone. Last time I had it, it was tucked into my jeans' pocket. The ones I wore yesterday to the club and later discarded in the bathroom. Hopefully, Rosa didn't wash them—with my phone! Thankfully, she didn't. I find it sitting on the kitchen counter with the few pounds I had in my pockets.

I slip the money into my pocket again and slump on the couch, unlocking my phone's display and skimming through what looks like seven hundred messages. Tanja obviously panicked a wee bit last night. There are a few missed calls from Felix, too. But that makes up only about five percent of what's there. I call Tanja first.

It doesn't even ring on my end before she immediately bellows into the phone, "Raff?"

"Tanja?" I reply with skepticism. Apparently, her hysteria hasn't calmed yet.

"Are you all right? Are you home? Why the hell did you turn off your phone last night? Nah, don't explain, I know why. But— *Damnit, Raffael*!"

Despite feeling all over the place emotionally after last night, her storm of words makes me chuckle. I tip to the side, lying on my back, and stack my feet on the backrest of the L-shaped couch. "Yeah, I'm home. And fine." The rest is something I'd rather not talk about. "What happened at eleven o'clock this morning? Your messages stopped as if someone hacked off your hands. Did you finally fall asleep?"

"No. I called Sebastian," she mutters. Her tone dead serious.

I almost choke on my spit. "Oh."

"He sent me a message sometime around dawn saying that you'll come around," Tanja murmurs huffily. "Do you even know what it's like to worry about a friend all night? Maybe I should give you a bit of that treatment one day just for revenge."

"I'm sorry..." I squeeze my eyes shut and pinch the bridge of my nose because I really do feel bad. It wasn't nice of me to leave her standing at the curb as I raced off from the club. But I wasn't in the mood to talk. Or to be with anyone. Half an hour later, when Sebastian walked into my home, proved just how well that hadn't worked out for me. "Things are just...overwhelming right now."

Two seconds pass, and then Tanja's sorrowful sigh drifts across the airwaves. She quietly replies, "I know." Another much longer pause follows. "So, what do you want to do now?"

I groan. "I wish you'd come over so I can fuck Sebastian out of my mind."

"Yeah, sorry, sweetie. That's not gonna happen." She chuckles. Of course, she would say that. But her laugh irritates me.

"Why not?"

"For one, you don't want to *fuck* me. I'm not who you need, even if I'm wearing Sebastian's t-shirt. And two... He asked me not to do that for a while."

I frown, staring at the blue sky outside the window. "Wearing his t-shirt?"

"Coming to your playroom, dummy." I can hear the eye-roll in her tone, but her voice softens almost instantly. "Sebastian said you might ask me to try and put your world back in order. He doubts it'll work. And I think he's right."

"And *I* think you two should stop colluding!"

"Raff..."

I sigh.

"You know," she continues, "I don't care for what he did in the club yesterday, but I'm pretty sure he likes you. A lot. And you and I both know that you like him, too."

I chew my bottom lip.

"Right?" she asks.

I suck on my teeth.

"Am I right, Raff?"

I stay silent.

"Come on, Raffael. You do!"

Eventually, I huff out an annoyed breath. "Yeah, I do." Now, she turns quiet, but I can almost *hear* her stupid grin in the silence. Witch! "Did he also tell you that he wants to take me somewhere this weekend?" I murmur. "We're supposed to stay overnight."

"No. Where are you going?"

"He didn't say. And I don't know if I want to."

"Sure, you do. Surprises are great."

"I hate them." And she knows it. "Dealing with him is so damn hard, especially when he makes me go against every bit of order in my life."

"You can't always control everything," she tells me, but I don't believe it. "You need to let go sometimes and open up. He's good for you."

I pout and frown and blow out another sulky breath. "He's good at destroying worlds."

Tanja's laugh rings in my ear. "Sweetie, it's time to loosen that knot of control in your mind."

"I can't."

"Yes, you can." A door slams shut on her side of the conversation as though she just left her apartment. "Don't go anywhere. I'm coming over."

I let a frisky grin enter my voice. "To fuck?"

"No, stupid." And then there's the silence that says she hung up.

I drop my hand with the phone and then send a text to Felix, telling him that Tanja is on her way over, and asking if he wants to join us. Sadly, he's visiting with his parents and won't be back until the evening. But he tells me to ask Tanja if she wants to do something later this week. A movie, perhaps. I like the idea because there's a new slasher flick I want to see.

When Tanja rings the bell, I rise from the couch and let her in. She kisses me on the cheek, and I briefly put one arm around her before closing the door as she slips out of her shoes. Since she's wearing jeans and a dark red *The Umbrella Academy* sweatshirt instead of some sexy outfit, it's clear she was serious about no screwing for a while. A small part of me realizes that I'm actually happy about that.

Tanja brought a backpack with her, which she tosses on the couch and then grabs a soda from the fridge. I quietly follow her to the kitchen island and take a seat on one of the three stools there. With my chin braced in my hands, I blow out a deep breath as I wait.

When she turns around, she fakes a pout and mirrors my pose on the opposite side of the counter.

"Why so serious?"

I roll my eyes but chuckle. "Don't go Joker on me, Hello Kitty."

Tanja grins and then takes a sip of her soda while she heads back into the living room. I turn my head to watch her. When she lowers to the floor near the coffee table and pats the surface for me to join her, I slide from the stool and go. Sitting on the floor alongside her, I ask, "Is there a reason we're not sitting on the couch?"

"Yep."

"Which is?"

With a traitorous smirk, she shrugs. "I just feel like doing something different today."

Head tilted, I give her a wry look. "Whatever you're trying won't work." Discovering that I'm into guys is a bit different than just breaking the rules of sitting on real furniture.

"Whaaat?" Her eyes fix on me as she takes another draught, all but splattering herself with the soft drink because she struggles to suppress another grin. "I'm not trying anything."

"Sure." Sarcasm leaks from my voice.

"I'm serious." She puts the can away and instead reaches for her backpack to pull something out. I wondered what she brought with her. It's a coloring book. What the heck? She also fetches a box of crayons. "We're just sitting down here because I want to do some art, and that's hard on the couch with this table being so low."

I cross my legs under the table and ask incredulously, "You want to color in this book?"

"Mm-hmm." She nods and starts using a blue crayon on the hat of a dwarf that sits in the middle of a sunflower field. For the next two minutes, she doesn't say a word or even look my way. She's entirely engrossed in her coloring. It's like I don't even exist to her.

Growling with irritation, I pick up the yellow crayon and start coloring one of the many blooms. But the silence gets annoying really fast, so I murmur after finishing a few more flowers, "Felix wants to go to the movies this week. You in?"

"Sure." She takes another color to shade the pants of the dwarf. "I can't go tomorrow or Wednesday, but Thursday would be great."

I nod, and then silence falls again. Seriously, this is like drawing lessons in primary school. Too little noise, too much time with my own thoughts. Since art is such a relaxing thing, it doesn't take long before Sebastian eats up the space in my mind again. Jeez. I hate it. Most of all because I begin to replay the moment in the hallway upstairs when we came out of different rooms, but with a totally new ending this time. I lick my lips. Involuntarily. Arrgh! I want to smack my head on the coffee table. Perhaps that would help shatter the wish to kiss Sebastian.

"Tanja?" I break the silence after some time without looking up. Half of the sunflower field is yellow, and the dwarf is in full color. "Have you heard about that Gay Pride Parade?"

"Yeah. It takes place in London every year. Why?"

Because I'm afraid that might be where Sebastian intends to take me this weekend. Although would he have said that we were staying overnight then? I keep that thought to myself and ask, "What kind of people do you think will be there?"

"Well...gay people."

"Ha. Ha." I roll my eyes. Tanja giggles, then takes

a purple crayon and starts to color one of the many sunflowers with it. My eyes pop wide, fixed on her assassination. "What the fuck are you doing?"

"I'm coloring this flower."

"Purple?" I snarl.

"Yes. It's my favorite color. So what?"

"It's a freaking sunflower. You can't color it purple."

"Sure, I can." I can hear the mischievousness in her voice, and she completely ignores my scowl. If that wasn't already bad enough, she actually stops after only one half and starts to color another random flower.

"Tanjaaa!" I snatch the crayon from her and finish the first one. She grabs it back and starts a goddamn third. Before she can do all the petals on this one, I shove her hand away and quickly color the rest of them yellow.

She throws her head back and laughs. "Raff, honey, you need to loosen up!" Then she picks a turquoise crayon and colors the sun with it. Jesus, I hate her.

Working on the flower field again, I cast sideways

glances at the sun every few seconds, grinding my teeth. I know she knows I'm watching her. And that I'm damning her to hell for this. Sadly, it doesn't stop her from doing more. No. The cow colors outside the lines next—on fucking purpose!

"How old are you? *Three?*" I explode.

One doesn't shade beyond the borders!

"Calm down, architect," she teases me. "No one ever died of a little color outside the lines."

"You want to torture me today, right? That's the only reason you came over."

She shakes her head no and grins. "Yes." Then she takes my hand and, moving my fingers, makes me color one of the clouds yellow. Did I mention that I hate her?

"You need to learn that it's okay to break the rules from time to time, Raff. The world will keep turning."

Yeah, that's what *she* thinks. But she's not the one facing a one hundred and eighty-degree turn in her life. "God, you have no idea what you're talking about—" A deep, weary sigh tears from me. "Shit, I don't even know how to behave around him.

Sebastian is so…he makes me nervous every time he's near."

"Because you're overthinking every second with him." Her fingers are warm on mine. Gentle. Yet unmerciful in their quest to ruin the picture and use colors that should never be. "Maybe just try to see him as someone like Felix for once. You wouldn't be so intimidated around *him*, would you."

Around Felix? No, I wouldn't. Because I'm not attracted to my best friend. My voice gets incredibly small. "But I don't want to be a…" I find her gaze, fearing that my voice will crack with the next word. "A *homo*. Gah, that sounds so terrible."

"Then don't call it that. Just say 'gay.'" She squeezes my hand a little tighter, the crayon still between our fingers. "Many people do. And there are actually lots of girls who find it absolutely sexy when men are bisexual."

No shit? My eyebrows tip into a curious frown. "Do *you*?"

With her gaze back on the book, Tanja continues coloring and murmurs, "Maybe." She shrugs, but the slight blush on her cheeks says she's serious. Who would have guessed?

Giving up on fighting her, I prop my left elbow on the table, rest my chin in my hand, and let her ruin the picture however she wants, abusing my hand and all the crayons. After we have a green sky, half a yellow and purple sunflower field, a red-skinned dwarf, and a pink tree, Tanja finally lets go of my hand. Bracing her forearms on the table, she leans over to kiss me on the cheek. "Don't be just one color, Raffael. Be the rainbow," she whispers.

Then she gets to her feet, grabs her backpack, and heads to the door, where she puts on her shoes. I guess the coloring book with its now deeper meaning is a gift to me. With the door already open and having moved halfway out, she smiles at me over her shoulder. "Ask Sebastian to tag along to the movies on Thursday."

It's not a suggestion, it's a damn order. And after being friends with her for most of my life, I know that *she*'ll do it if I don't.

I close the coloring book, blowing out a breath through my nose as I smile and then heave myself onto the couch.

Purple sunflowers? Crazy girl.

With the soles of my feet braced against the edge of the table, I reopen the conversation thread with Felix and confirm Thursday for the movies. Then I close WhatsApp, about to turn off the display, but my thumb hovers. The instant I even *think* about how to invite Sebastian to join us, a colony of invisible ladybugs swarms over my skin. The fucking crawlers are everywhere. I hate goosebumps.

Deep inhale. Long exhale.

Lips compressed, I go back to WhatsApp and open the third chat on the list, scrolling down to the very bottom. The words of our last conversation from two days ago cause the corners of my lips to twitch up a little.

Me

Night, Bash.

Sebastian

Night, Iceland

P.S. Your fingers felt amazing on my skin today.

It felt amazing to touch him. Last night in the playroom—fucking his mouth—was something I never dared to dream of before. But tracing the lines of the tattoos on his arms and chest in that incredibly tender moment we shared is what I still fantasize about when I close my eyes.

I close my eyes *now*, and I can almost smell Sebastian's scent, feel him next to me on the couch again.

Wanting to keep the warm feeling that's started to grow in my chest, I type a message to him.

Me

Are you serious? About going away this weekend.

For minutes on end, I stare at the two checks beside the text that refuse to turn blue. It's frustrating. Then again, it's Sunday. Maybe he's working at the gym and doesn't have his phone. To keep busy, I head to the kitchen and eat a few bites of the lasagna that Rosa and I had left over from lunch, but my gaze remains glued to the display of my phone on the coffee table.

A wave of adrenaline pushes through my veins when the gentle rumble of my smartphone on the glass top finally sounds out across the room. The tiny light on the upper left corner blinks blue.

Slowly, I pull the fork out of my mouth but stay rooted to the kitchen floor for several long seconds. Then I close the plastic container, put the lasagna back into the fridge, and return to the living room. With my phone in my hands, I slump on the couch and smile at his words.

Sebastian

I'm always serious when it comes to you.

Me

Where are we going?

Sebastian

Surprise. But you'll like it.

Me

Have a few more details for me, perhaps? When do we start off? Do I need something special to wear, like a suit? Safety equipment? Hiking shoes?

Sebastian

You don't need pajamas.

Me

Jeez, you're so fucking funny.

Sebastian

:-) I'll pick you up Saturday morning at ten.

Saturday morning is a long time to wait. I bite my bottom lip. Suddenly, I really want him to tag along to the movies with us on Thursday. Ah, what the hell...

Me

Do you have plans on Thursday?

Sebastian

Gym until noon. No plans after that. Why? Are you asking me for a date? :P

I roll my eyes but grin—rather stupidly.

Me

Sort of.

Sebastian

Go on.

Me

Felix wants to go to the cinema. Tanja wants you to come along.

Sebastian

What do YOU want?

Deep breath.
"*Be the rainbow,*" Tanja said.

Me

I think it would be nice to see you again before the weekend.

Sebastian

It sure would.

Me

But I'm not sharing my popcorn!

Sebastian

As long as you're sharing your drink...

Me

I just might...

Sebastian

Then you can tell Tanja that I'm happy to come.

I put the phone aside and rub my hands over my face, sighing into the tent of fingers I placed over my mouth and nose. Jesus Christ.

CHAPTER 4

Sebastian

It smells like warm popcorn and nachos with cheese dip, even this early in the afternoon when the cinema is still mostly empty. Raffael wrote to me yesterday and said that we're going to the first showing of the day because Tanja doesn't like watching slasher films too late. *Nightmares* was the official excuse. Like fuck. I'm pretty sure it was Raff's idea. Because at this time of day, the odds are good that we'll be alone in the theater, and no one will see him sitting next to me.

His panic is sort of sweet.

But the look he gives me from across the hallway

right now is Nordic fire.

With his hands in the pockets of his black skater pants, and the tips of his blond hair grazing his left eyebrow, he's been leaning against the wall staring at me for the last two minutes. I lean against the opposite wall, ten feet of deep red carpet between us, and appreciate the view.

When we met up a few minutes ago, Felix collected the money for the tickets so he could buy them in a bundle and then headed off. Of course, Raffael picked the spot farthest away from me to wait for Felix and Tanja to return. It made me chuckle. But his intense gaze keeps me rooted to my spot. Going slow means giving him the chance to decide when he's ready to come closer. I'm fine just staring into each other's eyes right now.

Raffael wears the t-shirt he wore on the racing night again, the vertically parted white and black one. There's some random printed text in red in a square box on the left side of his chest, and another a little lower on the right. I wonder if he'll give me the chance to get close enough to read it tonight. Regardless, I deem this shirt my favorite. Maybe out of sentimentality. He wore it when we kissed for the first time.

It's funny how you could make out with a hundred different people in your life and not remember how any of those kisses felt. But when you touch the lips of that one special person, you never forget.

Thumbs tucked through the belt loops of my jeans, I angle one leg and place the sole of my shoe against the wall behind me. A lopsided grin slips before I ask, "So...is there a seating order today that cages you in between your friends? Or do you dare sit next to me?"

I expect him to immediately look all over the place, making sure no one heard. But Raffael surprises me. His gaze doesn't waver an inch, and an easy shrug rolls off his shoulder. "How will I share my drink with you if I don't sit next to you?" And then a tiny smile follows.

Holy fuck! I'm in love.

Raff draws in a somewhat deep breath that straightens his spine. He pushes away from the wall and slowly draws closer, working his bottom lip between his teeth, but bravely holding my stare. A single foot away from me, he finally breaks eye contact as he spins and leans with his back against the wall right next to me. Stunned, I slowly turn my head to the side.

"I'm starting to worry," I say, only half-joking about it.

"Don't." He blinks, then keeps his eyes lowered, fixing on the gray pattern of the dark red carpet. "I'm just trying to be..." A deep breath interrupts his words, and he closes his eyes. "...open. Tanja can be really persistent. She's been at my place quite a few times since Sunday."

She has? My lips stay sealed, and I remain planted against the wall. At my silence, Raff turns to me. "Living room," he reassures me quietly, no doubt reading my thoughts. Just as I push the images of them fucking in the playroom aside, he continues. "She forced me into a pot of rainbows. Repeatedly. We've done a lot of coloring this week."

Ah...yes. That makes totally no sense to me. But to him, it obviously does, and that's all I need. I like the change in him, however subtle it may be.

"Courage suits you," I say in a warm voice. Then I laugh. "But the excuse with Tanja's nightmares is bullshit. You're setting up your own environment to test your limits."

Raffael grins, focusing on the floor once more. "Could be that I am."

I knock my elbow against his arm gently and tell him, "That's okay." I know how hard it is for him to expand the territory where he feels comfortable being seen with a guy. Sure, I loved those hours in his apartment when we were by ourselves—the time with him on the couch even more than in the playroom truth be told. But it's also nice to do things outside his home. Together.

That he's trying means a hell of a lot...to me.

Moments later, his friends come back from the counter, and Felix holds a fan of four tickets. I pick the one on the far left, and Raffael takes the very next one. There's still a few minutes before the movie begins, and when Tanja announces that she's dashing to the loo before we go inside, I walk with her to the restrooms.

The other two amble off to the kiosk, and I hear

Raffael's not-so-subtle tease from behind us. "Girls... Always have to go to the bathroom together."

Sorry, *what*? A laugh escapes me as I spin around before the corner, lifting my hand to flip him off. But then I don't, because he stands there with his hands in his pockets and the cutest, brave little smile on his face.

I only notice that I stopped walking when Tanja hooks her arm through mine and pulls me around the bend. "Toilet's that way," she mocks me.

Rolling my eyes at myself, I chuckle and squeeze my arm to my side to keep her hand trapped. "Listen, I don't know what kind of shit you did with Raff this week, but I..." Somehow at a loss for how to continue, I shrug and draw my brows down, my head turned to her. "Thanks."

Her warm doe eyes move up to my face. "Raffael's a great guy. Someone special. I always want to see him happy." Before us, the hallway splits. The ladies' and gents' on opposite sides. Tanja stops and slips her hand away but keeps her smile. "And I think you *make* him happy."

I'm not quite sure if I do, at least not always, but I

really dig that carefree smile when he allows himself to let it out. It's an exhilarating feeling to be the one responsible for it.

Tanja disappears into the restroom on the right, and I take the door with the stick man. She's already back with the others when I return, bantering with Felix. Raffael has a popcorn bag in the crook of his arm, and a Sprite can in his hand. His gaze is glued to the phone in his other hand as he types something, his single thumb tapping. I know he said he wouldn't share his popcorn, but I can't resist briefly looping my arm around his neck and plucking a couple of kernels from the overfilled bag. My hold on him tightens as I pop them into my mouth.

Shit. Big mistake. I turn away from him and spit the mouthful into the trash can by the wall. "Sheesh, you like the sweet type of popcorn?"

Raffael puts his phone away and casts me a scornful grin. "That will teach you not to touch my food."

With a scrunched-up face, I lift my hands in surrender. "Never again, I swear."

He pulls up the hem of his t-shirt and thoroughly

rubs the top of the Sprite can with it. His black pants ride low on his hips and show a strip of his Calvin Klein boxer briefs and an enticing bit of skin on his hard stomach. When the t-shirt falls again, I look up at the sound of carbonation as he opens the Sprite and then holds it out to me. "Want to wash away the taste?"

"I can think of a better way to change the taste in my mouth," I drawl, fixing his eyes as I accept the drink and take a sip.

Raffael's gaze drops to my mouth, and he wets his lips with his tongue. Probably an unconscious movement but...yep, that's exactly what I was thinking about.

"Come on, guys," Tanja interrupts our moment, dragging Felix past us. "We should get to our seats. I want to see the trailers, too."

I carry the Sprite into the cinema hall and put it into the holder between Raffael's and my seat as we sit down in the very last row. Looks like we're pretty much alone in here, apart from three teenagers who've claimed spots five rows in front of us and animatedly talk with one another. Felix lowers into the chair on Raffael's left, and Tanja takes the outer seat next to him.

The trailers are already running, and five minutes later, the lights dim more as the film begins. I scoot deep into my lounge chair and focus on the screen. The spooky opening melody eventually silences the kids, and a familiar tension overtakes the room. I hardly ever go to the movies, but if I do, it's almost always to watch a horror film.

Raffael doesn't seem to be interested in the opening at all. For the first quarter of an hour, he's deeply involved with his popcorn, shoveling handfuls of it into his mouth. I watch him from the corner of my eye, and from time to time, turn my head to look at him directly. "What?" he asks quietly around a mouthful, lifting his brows as he obviously feels disturbed by my fascination. Chuckling, I just shake my head and then watch the young woman on screen run into her stalker. Raffael misses it entirely as he tips the whole bag with the remaining crumbs into his mouth. Somebody loves his sweet popcorn.

He scrunches up the paper bag and stuffs it into the holder, replacing the Sprite. After he takes a deep draught, I grab the soda from him and drink from it, too. He only left me a mouthful, so I put the empty can into the holder on my other side and then place my left hand on the armrest between us. The thing is wide enough for three arms, but Raffael immediately pulls his away when our elbows accidentally touch. It was probably reflex, yet it irritates me a little, and I frown at his right thigh, where his fingers now claw into the fabric of his pants.

Two steps forward, one step back.

I shouldn't bother because he's making some great progress. But to have him sitting next to me for another hour, so close without body contact, ruins the fun of the afternoon for me a wee bit.

My fingers itch to just reach over and lace with his. Except that would only make matters worse. For him and, in the long run, for me, too. So, I just expel a deep sigh and leave my hand where it is.

"I'm sorry..." His quiet words drift to me and make my head snap around to him. His sad eyes are focused straight on me as if he'd been watching me glare at his lap. Something uncomfortable lodges in my throat because now *I*'m actually sorry. I hold his stare, blinking slowly with my lips compressed. Lesson learned. No fast movements around him today.

His throat twitches as he swallows, and then he turns front to follow the action on the screen again. Several seconds later, I do the same. Soon, something close to my arm catches my attention, however. Without moving my head this time, I just look down and smile slightly. Raffael laid his forearm back on the armrest, *almost* touching mine.

I keep utterly still, only watching how his fingers start to drum a nervous beat on the upholstered arm. They inch toward mine. I lick my lips, my grin growing a little wider.

Now, what are you going to do, Iceland?

Time seems frozen for seconds on end. If I took his hand and laced our fingers, I know he would let me. If somebody dared him to do it, he would, too. But going beyond his rules and regulations for no other reason than *wanting* to touch me is a whole different kind of endeavor for Raffael. One that obviously takes him to his limits.

Slowly, I twist my hand around so my open palm

faces up. I'm not going to take the decision away from him but I can give him a subtle invitation. He doesn't even try to hide that he's concentrating on what's going on between us instead of the movie. I can see it from the corner of my eye.

His right leg begins to teeter as his fingers crawl closer to mine, millimeter by fucking millimeter. They lift from the armrest in slow-motion until they finally hover just an inch above my palm. Goddammit, my heart starts to pound, matching the rhythm his rocking knee provides.

Come on, Raff, you're almost there. Just a little bit closer.

I hold my breath. His middle finger is the first to lower, brushing my skin with the faintest touch. But the very next instant, he jerks his arm away, throwing both his hands over his face. The whine that drifts through his fingers is pathetic and possibly the sweetest sound I've heard all week.

Laughing, I clap a hand on his thigh, just briefly, and then lean close to him. "If only you knew, snowflake..." I rasp, brushing his ear with my lips intentionally.

Raffael lowers his hands and sighs deeply. "This is...just so *hard*," he says quietly. He looks miserable, clearly unable to get over himself.

Soon, we'll be spending two entire days together, even sleeping in the same room. There'll be plenty of time to try again.

I recline in my seat, lacing my fingers over my stomach as I bring my attention back to the screen. Several moments later, however, I move my legs a little farther apart, touching his right knee gently with my left. I turn my head slightly and find his eyes, giving him a soft smile. Raffael smiles back. And that's that.

We stay like that until the end of the film. No more nervous finger drumming, no more teetering legs. When the movie is over, and it's time to leave, I almost regret the past couple of hours flying by so fast.

Luckily, Felix suggests that we have a drink at the pub around the corner before we go home. So, we all file around a small table with a marble top. An animated conversation about the movie has started up between Felix and Tanja by the time we sit down and place our orders. Occasionally, I throw in my two pennies' worth. Still, most of the time, I'm distracted by observing Raffael, who seems to have retreated into a quiet world of his own. When the waitress brings our warm drinks and Felix's lemon soda, Iceland doesn't pay attention to either of us. Instead, he thanks her with a smile and then pulls the cup on the saucer toward him.

While I drink my espresso black, Tanja tips half a packet of sugar into her green tea then hands the rest to Raffael without invitation or stopping her rant regarding the slasher movie. Still not listening, Raff pours the other half of her sugar and one of his own into his cappuccino. His thoughtful gaze wanders around the cup, probably in search of another. The pub obviously economizes with the supplies.

His brows tip together in a cute, disappointed way, coaxing my smile. I pick the single sugar sachet from my saucer and slowly push it across the table to him with two fingers.

Raffael's hand freezes in the motion of stirring his coffee when he sees the sugar packet coming. Reluctantly, he lets go of the spoon and reaches out to accept the sachet, offering me a tiny grin as he slowly pulls it toward him the rest of the way. He shakes the packet twice to get one corner free of crystals to tear it open, then he pours the entire load into this already much too sweet cappuccino. Stirring again with the little silver spoon, his face eases into a content and relaxed expression. He takes a sip and then leans back, apparently ready to notice the rest of the world now.

"Oh my gosh," Tanja blurts out, squeezing a little bit of juice from a lemon wedge into her tea. "I thought I was going to pee my pants when he went looking for the little girl in the house at the beginning."

Raff tilts his head and frowns at his two best friends. "There was a little girl?"

Both of them fall silent and stare at him as if he just announced that he was going to move to the North Pole. I crack up laughing. "Oh, man, Iceland, I love the way you do everything with a devotion to an extreme degree."

The whisper of a blush crosses his cheekbones because he remembers perfectly well what distracted him so badly that he completely missed the first murder in the film.

Eventually, Tanja shakes her head, and Felix runs a hand through his ginger hair before the two slip back into their conversation. They analyze everything about the plot and go back and forth regarding what they would have done differently. It's funny to listen to them as they seem to be of opposing opinions on every fucking detail. Yet they have a passion for each other that's almost tangible across the table. I wonder if I'm the only one who notices it.

Sometime later, as we all stand outside the pub and say goodbye, I briefly hug Tanja and then clasp hands with Felix. Raffael is the last one I turn to. Suddenly, there's an uneasy silence between us again. A hug would be too much, but bumping fists just doesn't feel right. Our friendship is somewhere in between that I find hard to place right now. So, at a loss for options, I finally tuck my hands into my jeans' pockets and tilt my head with a smirk. "See you on Saturday."

Raff gives a slow, terse nod without saying a word. But the corners of his lips twitch a little in a smile.

That's all I can ask for. Happy, I leave.

*

On Saturday morning, I pack a few clothes into a duffle bag and then go hunting for the dark blue hoodie I borrowed from Raff last weekend. Since I only wore it a couple of hours that evening, I didn't see the need to wash it before returning it to its owner. But the damn thing obviously wants to play hide and seek.

After several long minutes and some unholy cussing, I finally find it draped over one of the two high stools at the kitchen bar where I usually eat instead of sitting alone at the table. I grab it along with the car keys, switch off all the lights in my seventy-four square-meter apartment, lock the door, and then head down the single flight of stairs to leave the building.

My car sleeps at the end of the road, but after I toss the duffle into the trunk and Raff's hoodie on the passenger seat, it awakens to life with a welcoming roar. Saturday morning traffic is a pain in the ass, so I planned in some extra time for the ride to Mayfair. I arrive at Raffael's home at three past ten.

Underground car park. I shoot him the message through WhatsApp and hope he's ready. He sends back a thumbs-up emoji really fast. No invitation to come upstairs probably means he's on his way down. Good. I get out of the car and wait for him, leaning against the door, my hands stuffed into the pockets of my baggy shorts.

Two minutes later, a single chime sounds from the elevator as the door opens. Raffael steps out, wearing one of his large white hockey shirts over blue jeans. A worn-out black backpack hangs over his right shoulder. As he walks up to me, not a single muscle in his face twitches, but his eyes are focused intensely on mine. He stops a couple of feet away.

I straighten from the car and place one hand on the door handle. "Are you ready?"

The snowflake pulls his ice-blue sunglasses from his head and slides them down over his eyes. They make him look closed-off yet damn hot.

"Let's go," he says, then his lips stretch into a

warm, wide grin, and I want to eat him up.

CHAPTER 5

Raffael

Fuck, I'm a nervous wreck this morning. Sitting on a barstool in the kitchen, Felix laughs at me while I crouch on the floor and clean up the mess I made as the coffee mug slipped through my fingers. He's been around since a quarter past eight, right after he woke me with a message that he'd like to talk to me before I head off for my weekend with Sebastian.

I only hope it's not a conversation about safe sex with a man, or I may have to kill him and bury his body in the woods.

"I've never seen you this edgy before," he says, rubbing his chin, his eyes bearing an amused gleam.

"If I didn't know any better, I'd say you're head over heels for the guy."

I spear him with a glare over my shoulder, but I don't contradict him.

Intrigue softens his face. "So, you are..."

A deep sigh escapes me as I rise from the floor and toss the shards of the mug into the trash, then I turn to him and confess, "There's just something about Sebastian that makes me really antsy." Excited. Thrilled. Happy. Melancholic. All at the same time. If this is how you should feel when you're falling for someone, then maybe I am.

"Hey, that's okay. It's great!" He lifts the black-and-white-striped coffee mug in a toasting gesture. "It's about time you found someone who creeps under your skin." The gleam in his hazel eyes is honest, but there's something else underneath that I can't quite place. Felix sets his mug down without drinking and then pulls down the collar of his green sweatshirt, scratching at his neck. He always does that when he feels uncomfortable about something. I take a step back and hoist myself up onto the kitchen counter, tilting my head. I imagine this is where the real conversation will begin.

"If you had asked me three weeks ago, I'd never have even dared to believe that you were interested in guys. And still, on some level it calms me, to be honest." Felix throws me a little off guard with that statement.

"Why?" I demand.

He takes a draught of coffee and then clears his throat, his gaze lowered to the top of the kitchen island. "Sharing Tanja has recently become somewhat exhausting."

My eyebrows arch with surprise until he glances at me again. Cautious.

"I kind of like her. Like really, *really* like her," he murmurs.

As do I. But this sounds as if one of us is truly in *love* with her. I didn't see this coming at all.

Gripping the edge of the counter, I narrow my eyes at my best friend in the world. "Why the fuck didn't you say something?"

He gives me a helpless shrug.

"Does Tanja know how you feel?"

Felix licks his lips and, after a moment, shakes his

head. "She always seemed happy with how things were between the three of us. I didn't want to take you away from her. Or her from you. I don't know." His face scrunches into a grimace as he glares into his mug. "I didn't want to ruin our special friendship by making things complicated."

"Complicated?" I blow out a cynical breath. "Hell, I can probably tell you a thing or two about that."

"Exactly." He wraps his fingers around the mug as if he needs something to hold onto to continue the conversation. "You've got your own...*love story* going on right now. Things are changing all by themselves, and Tanja finally came to realize that she won't have both of us forever and ever. I don't think she would have been able to decide between us because there was just *always* the three of us."

He's right. We've been a trio for a long time. And we'd probably have stayed that way for the next fifty years if an outsider hadn't come in to cause a shift in our strange, amazing friendship triangle. Honestly, it could have hit any of us. That it happened to me was mere coincidence.

Legs dangling, I stare at my toes. "So, when are

you going to talk to her about it?"

"I thought maybe this weekend. I just wanted to speak with you first and see if it's okay."

Somewhat incredulous, I snap my head up. "That you ask her to be exclusive with you?"

Felix nods. "I just wasn't sure if you were ready to give her up."

My chin drops. "If you'd said even one word, dipshit, I'd have stopped fucking around with her the very first day! Even before Sebastian came into my life and turned everything upside down. You know I love her. But all of us know that I never *loved* her." Whereas Felix does, and that's wonderful. They're the perfect fit. Felix will be good to Tanja. And even though I know she's always had romantic feelings for me—which I could never return—she feels exactly the same for Felix.

I slide down from the counter and brace myself on my hands on the kitchen island in front of him, nailing him with a meaningful stare. "Go for it."

For a short moment, Felix searches my eyes. Then a determined grin curves his lips. "I will." He gets down from the barstool and glances at the clock on the wall as he heads to the door. It's quarter to ten. "And will you?"

Speaking about Tanja has calmed me some over the past few minutes. And even though the ladybugs are back, prickling my skin, I nod firmly as I see him out. I had an entire week to get ready for this trip. After the time with Sebastian in the movies on Thursday, I was getting more and more excited for this weekend to finally begin.

We say goodbye, smack hands, then I close the door behind him and walk back to the living room. I pick up my sunglasses from the coffee table and slip them onto my head for later. Then I slump on the cushions next to my black backpack filled with a few changes of clothes, a toothbrush, and the charging cable for my cell phone.

Minutes later, my phone chimes out with directions to where Sebastian is waiting for me. My stomach twists into knots, but my heart performs a flip of anticipation.

I sling the backpack over my shoulder and take the private elevator straight to the underground car park. Inside, I lean against the back wall and grip the metal bar hard with both hands. Watching the numbers of the floors flash one by one, counting down from nine, only makes me more anxious. Finally, I just glance at my toes and wait for the ride to stop.

With a low ding, the door slides open. I take a deep breath before I lift my head and find Sebastian leaning against his white Honda, his gaze trained on me. The sight of him does several things to me at once. It makes me want to grin because, fuck, he looks gorgeous in a black hoodie and beige jeans shorts. His legs are tanned nicely, something my pale skin never does, and his dark red shoes flash. The Nike cap he wears is flipped around on his head like usual, and his chestnut eyes gleam wickedly.

Squaring my shoulders, I walk toward him, feeling my heart rate increase with every step.

Sebastian pushes off the car. "Are you ready?"

I like the soft, confident sound of his voice. It's infectious.

I slide the sunglasses down over my eyes and let them tint the world in a mysterious hue of dark ice. "Let's go," I reply and finally let the grin slip that has been building in me since the moment I received his message.

While he gets behind the steering wheel, I skirt the hood and open the door on the other side. As a surprise, my dark blue hoodie lies on the passenger seat. I grab it and push it into the backpack between my feet after climbing in. Sebastian's laundered shirt and t-shirt still sit on the chest of drawers in my bedroom. I didn't think about giving them back to him the entire week—nor do I now.

I buckle in as we move with the traffic, facing the sun. Still a little anxious, I let my knees tip together and apart several times. "Can you tell me now where we're going?"

His gaze slides my way, then he looks down at my legs and laughs. "Don't worry, I'm a good driver."

"Yeah, that's not what's making me nervous." A bout of cynicism threads through my tone. Somehow, I still feel a bit panicked that he's taking me to the Gay Pride Parade. It sort of sounds like fun, but part of me just doesn't want to go there.

My unease must be amusing to him because Sebastian grins. But as we cross Albert Bridge, he takes mercy on me. "We're going out of town. South."

I frown at the taillights in front of us. What's in South England? When I stalked him on the internet the first night we met, it said that he was born there and went to college there, too. "Eastbourne?" I ask. Is he actually taking me to his home? My heart stutters a little at the thought. For some reason, there was a picture of a nice hotel in the mountains in my mind the entire week.

He narrows his eyes on me in a quick sideways look. "Since you figured out where I work, I probably shouldn't be surprised that you also know where I come from, huh?"

"Facebook," I explain. "Why are we going to your hometown?"

"I want you to meet someone there." And, immediately, his expression warms again.

His ease isn't catching. I wipe my suddenly clammy hands on my jeans. Shit, it's far too early to get introduced to people in his life who are special. My voice turns hoarse. "Your family?"

"A small portion of it, yes." He smiles. "But, don't

worry, you won't have to answer any weird questions. One of them knows me better than any person in the world and is used to seeing me with guys. And the other is utterly unbiased."

His descriptions sound very much like people I might call Mom and Dad. Or Tanja and Felix... I don't know if any of that soothes me. The urge to cover my face with my hands and just crawl back into hiding overcomes me. I have to fight it really hard, but I do my best to keep cool and sink deeper into the seat, as far as the buckle harness allows anyway. Those things are usually really tight. Oddly, it gives me a small feeling of comfort—something I need right now.

The lines of houses in the city soon give way to green landscapes all around us. The open spaces let me breathe again and empty my mind. I tilt my head to the side and glance at the bright blue sky through the window. A small smile tugs at my lips. In Tanja's coloring book, the skies were green, pink, yellow, and red. Never blue.

"What do you think?" Sebastian breaks into my thoughts. "Who of us will win the race?"

"The one Elliot wants to stage between you and me?" I haven't thought about that all week.

He gives a curt nod.

"Well, if you drive like you're driving now...it'll be me," I taunt him.

Taking the jab gracefully and giving a laugh, Sebastian presses down on the accelerator so the car flies down the road. The force of the acceleration presses me into the seat, and I love it. It's precisely how you should drive a car.

Closing my eyes, I heave a deep sigh. It's then that I pay attention to the subtle scent in the car for the first time today. Sun-warmed skin beneath a layer of musky shower gel. Maybe that's how rainbows smell.

Turning my head to the side, I take in Sebastian's profile as he drives. He's focused on the empty rural road ahead of us but drives with an ease that makes me wonder if he's lost in his own thoughts at the moment. One of his hands rests on the steering wheel, and the other cups the gear shift. Even from just the skin and muscle tone visible, one can see that he's got a natural, muscular build. Something I would only reach if I started knocking back anabolic steroids. I don't envy him. But I do enjoy the view.

He notices my stare. "Is everything okay?" he demands with a soft tone.

I don't answer immediately because I want to analyze the feeling creeping up inside me first. The acute panic is gone. Whatever comes this weekend, I think I'm strong enough to face it. Sebastian doesn't always use the gentlest of ways to get what he wants, and in some instances, he actually *forced* my eyes open with merciless brutality. But it ultimately put me on a path I've come to like because it's one we're on together. I'm not ready to tell the rest of the world yet that I've started falling for a guy, but it's okay to admit it to myself.

"Yes," I finally tell him.

Sebastian's brows quirk with curiosity as he turns to me, and I believe it's because I took so long to answer. He must see something in my eyes, though, because he smiles with a bit of wonder before he faces front again.

Now that I know where we're headed, pictures form in my mind of how this weekend will go. Meals at a big table with a couple probably in their mid-fifties. *Mr. & Mrs. Rhyse* printed on the doormat. Perhaps a dog barking inside the...what? Apartment? House? Even though I'm looking forward to spending the time with Sebastian, the thought of being around other people creates an oppressive feeling in my gut. If he wants to hang out together more often in the future, we really need to speak about vacation preferences.

An insecure croak sneaks into my voice. "How will you introduce me to your family?" If, at any point during this weekend, the word *boyfriend* drops, I'll likely take the first train home and delete his number from my phone.

"Raffael, the gay," he deadpans and then cracks up when I roll my eyes and punch his arm.

"Not funny," I growl.

Sebastian fights his grin and then finally swallows it. "I'm sorry." He sounds so soft now that I actually believe him. "How would you like to be introduced?" he asks me.

I have no idea what to say.

If they really are used to seeing him with other men, it makes me uneasy that they would think I'm into guys from the very first *hello.* At a loss, I shrug.

"Would it be okay if I tell them that you're..."—he looks at me, his face still warm and understanding—"a friend?"

"One that you aren't fucking?"

His lips curve into a smirk. "You want me to say that?"

"No!"

He laughs again and then places his hand on my thigh to reassure me. He leaves it there for much too long, but it's not at all uncomfortable, so I tolerate it. "Don't worry, Iceland," he says while his thumb strokes back and forth. "I'll be decent when I introduce you."

It's so much easier to let touches happen when he initiates them. Every time I think about reaching out and trying something, my heart rate lurches into the red zone of danger. I feel like a fucking coward. When Sebastian takes his hand away to place it back on the gear shift, I miss the sensation of his warm fingers on my jeans almost immediately.

"Felix came to my place this morning," I tell him just to keep the conversation going and because I like hearing him talk. "We spoke about him and Tanja."

"Are they in a relationship now?"

His question is so easy, so dead-on, that my gaze flies back to him in wonder. "No. But I think they will be soon. Felix wants to ask her to be exclusive."

He nods.

"You're not surprised?"

"No." He turns his frown on me. "Are you?"

"A little. I didn't see it coming."

"I bet Tanja didn't either."

"But you did…?"

He deliberates a bit before he speaks. "Do you know the frog in boiling water principle?"

My brows tip into a V. "Yes." Put a frog into boiling water, and it'll jump right out. Put it in cold water and then slowly heat the pot, and the frog will stay until it's cooked.

"I guess it's like that with the three of you." An easy smile turns the corners of his mouth up as he tilts his head to me for a moment and then concentrates on the road again. "Sometimes, it's easier for an outsider to notice…that the water is hot."

For several seconds, I stare at the side of his face and then swallow. "We're not talking about Tanja and Felix anymore, are we?"

With his grin still in place, he quickly arches his eyebrows, casting me a meaningful look.

Yeah. I've been the frog in slowly heating water all my life.

CHAPTER 6

Raffael

As we cross the borders of Eastbourne, a slight nervousness takes root in my stomach. I glue my gaze to the window as I watch the picturesque suburbs pass by. Everything is beautiful and green here. Gorgeous single-family homes with big gardens line the street, and kids ride their bikes on the sidewalk.

The core of Eastbourne closer to the shore is a bit more crowded with taller apartment buildings, but we drive through and take a right turn toward the outskirts of town again. A warm sea breeze tickles my nose as I roll down the window. Above us, seagulls draw circles in the sky.

Sebastian slows the car in a cozy neighborhood and then parks in front of an adorable white house with cappuccino-brown shutters and a wooden door. I take off my sunglasses and put them into my backpack while he throws his cap onto the back seat and runs a hand through his hair. He gets out of the car first. I take a moment to compose myself before I follow.

Stretching my stiff back and shoulders from the long drive, I turn around, drinking in the beauty of the place. The enormous front garden stretches around to the back of the structure. From what I can make out from here, there's no fence behind the house. There is a meadow that stretches into the wilderness, and a neat little wooded area in the distance.

"You grew up here?" I ask Sebastian.

He removes his duffle bag from the trunk. "Yep. I lived in a flat in the center of town for a couple of years after I turned twenty, but I moved back in three years ago and stayed until I went to London last winter."

Picking up my backpack from the floor in front of the passenger seat, I wonder how hard it was for him to leave such an enchanting place. Then again, I'm really happy he did. If he hadn't, we never would have met.

Sebastian slings his bag over a shoulder, and I do the same with my backpack, slamming the door shut. "Come on," he says with a smile as he walks through the gate in the low, white picket fence. I follow a little reluctantly. A stone path winds through the front garden leading to the house. We pass a huge cedar tree on the left. Planters with multi-colored flowers hang in front of each window—a paradise for the many butterflies that reflect the sunlight like dewdrops in the morning.

We're halfway through the garden when the front door opens. I swallow. A young woman with black, shoulder-length hair and a dark blue summer dress welcomes us from the doorstep. I recognize the woman's face immediately. She's the one from the picture on Sebastian's phone. Only, in that shot, she held a toddler.

"Hi, Bash!" she cheers, opening her arms.

Sebastian drops his bag. "Come here, you!" He pulls her into a tight hug, lifting her from the two steps in front of the door. When he puts her back on her feet, her beaming gaze finds me.

"My sister, Claudia," Sebastian introduces me to her and then dons a wide, wicked grin before he lays an arm around my shoulders and looks at her again. "Raff, the gay."

My jaw drops. Tilting my head back, I rub my hands over my face and groan. Jesus Christ!

Laughing, Sebastian lets go of me and then carries his bag inside. In the meantime, I take a deep breath and face our host. She holds out a delicate hand, offering me a smile so warm and soft it's like the sunlight on the butterflies' wings. "Hello, Raffael. Don't mind my little brother. He was born an idiot, and no one had the heart to drown him in the ocean."

"Stop complaining!" Sebastian's amused voice drifts from inside the house. "You had several chances when we were kids. But I was the cutest baby, and you loved me too much to get rid of me."

Giggling, Claudia shrugs and wrinkles her nose.

"That's true," she mouths to me while I squeeze her hand. "Come on in. I've got a plate with sandwiches in the kitchen. I didn't know what you like, so I made the lot."

"Thanks," I say, following her into the sun-flooded house. "But that wasn't necessary, really." The small space behind the door is filled with a coat rack and a chest of drawers that holds a crystal vase with a bunch of sunflowers in it. They're all yellow, of course, which makes me smile because it reminds me of my many hours with Tanja and the fight over greens skies and purple sunflowers.

We head to the living area adjacent to the kitchen through a wide, arched break in the wall. Off-white tiles cover the entire floor of the ground level, and the white walls make the space look even bigger. Lots of pictures, paintings, and shelves hang on the walls, and a gentle sea breeze blows in, carrying the scents of the many flowers outside the open windows.

I put my backpack on the floor beside the blue-gray couch that seems to be the home of the entire *Winnie the Pooh* gang and some other random stuffed animals like a panda and an opalescent sea turtle. From there, I follow Claudia into the kitchen where Sebastian leans with his hip against the white kitchen island. He's already shoveled the first of a pyramid of triangular-cut sandwiches into his mouth.

"Come and have one," Claudia offers again. "I'll cook dinner later this evening."

I'm so nervous that eating is the last thing I want to do right now, but I also don't want to be impolite. I pick up a ham salad half. After the first bite, I set it on the apple-green napkin Claudia hands me.

"Where is she?" Sebastian asks with a full mouth, checking the second arch in the wall that looks to lead to a hallway leading to the back part of the house.

"After-lunch nap." Claudia turns to me again. "Would you like something to drink? Sebastian said you—"

Her sentence gets cut off by her brother, who opens the fridge and tosses a Sprite can across the kitchen in my direction. Luckily, I catch it with both hands. He opens a Coke for himself and takes a sip. "You put her to sleep at"—he glances at his wristwatch—"twelve o'clock? Didn't you tell her that

I was coming?"

Claudia gives him a reprimanding glare and then takes a glass out of the cupboard. "If I'd told her that, she would've been waiting for you by the door since six this morning." Her friendly expression is for me as she sets the glass next to my soda. I don't know what Sebastian told her exactly, but she obviously thinks I'm not the type of person who drinks from a can. Again, not to be impolite, I smile with gratitude. I tap the top of the can to calm the bubbles from Sebastian's toss, and the soda fizzes as I pop the top and pour half the contents into the glass.

Sebastian rolls his eyes at me from behind his sister and then takes another draught from his Coke.

"How long does she nap these days?" Sebastian demands, inhaling the rest of his bacon sandwich.

Claudia shrugs but then her gaze gets caught on something by the entrance to the living room. Her face lights up with love. "Not as long as usual today, it seems."

Sebastian and I turn around at the same time and find a little girl in a white romper with bunnies on it standing in the arch. She clasps a stuffed raccoon to her chest with tiny hands, and behind the huge pacifier that covers half her face, a heartwarming smile makes her chubby cheeks puff out. Her blue eyes twinkle with delight.

"Hey, baby doll!" Sebastian blurts out. He skirts the kitchen island, rushes toward her, and lifts her into his arms. She drops the raccoon to free her hands and loops her arms around his neck, squeezing with all the strength a little princess can manage. "I missed you, too," he murmurs into her ear, stroking her silky blond locks that stand in riotous angles from her head.

"Is this your daughter?" I ask Claudia just to make conversation, but I can't tear my gaze away from the sweet scene across the room. The two are adorable together.

"Yes. Her name is Michelle. She just turned two a couple of months ago."

"Bash sing?" Michelle squeals behind her pacifier, flattening her hands to Sebastian's cheeks to make him look straight at her happy face.

"What, you want to sing *now*?" he replies and comes over to sit the baby on the kitchen island. She bobs her head with all the hope in the world. Her gem-like eyes don't let him out of her sight for even a second as he fetches his phone from his pocket, obviously searching for a song.

Sebastian cuts me a brief look and smirks. "You're gonna like this." Then he presses play on the cell and turns up the volume. *"Pow-Wow,"* he rasps along with the music as soon as the song begins. He pounces on the little girl like a wolf. She giggles, hunching her shoulders, and ducking her head. Five distinctive piano notes chime out next, giving away which song from Bon Jovi is obviously special to Sebastian and his niece. *It's My Life.*

Michelle has taste.

Sebastian sings the first line and grabs the toddler from the counter to hoist her up and make her sit on his shoulders. Holding both her hands tight beside his face, he dances across the room with her, and the hearty laughter of the child fills the house.

He goes down to his knees, causing Michelle to tip backward. Out of the corner of my eye, I catch Claudia clapping her hands over her mouth with anxiety, but Sebastian obviously knows what he's doing. I get the idea that he's done this many, many times with Michelle in the past.

After he straightens again, he comes forward and looks me in the eyes as he continues singing. His features and that of the girl in sync turn mean with the lyrics. With Michelle's baby hand in his, he pumps the air twice to the hard bass drum beat.

I'm falling in love. With a little girl—and her uncle.

He spins away from me and twists back to the middle of the room, both of them singing that it's 'Now or never', even though Michelle's singing sounds more like blaring some random vowels only.

The two have a blast, Sebastian spinning and spinning around. Michelle's head tips back, the pacifier sliding to the corner of her mouth because she's laughing so hard. At some point, she can't hold it any longer on the wild carrousel, and it goes flying through the room. When it rolls near my feet, I pick it up and wash it under the tap, then set it on the countertop next to my half-eaten sandwich.

"Bash, don't!" Claudia pleads, half laughing, half whining as she covers her eyes. "She just got out of bed."

That doesn't seem to bother either uncle or niece because Sebastian pulls her down from his shoulders, head-first, and then holds her up high above his face, singing up to her. Michelle giggles hard and tries to sing without choking from joy. Not a chance.

I don't have any siblings, but if I could be an uncle to anyone, I'd want it to be to a merry child like Michelle.

Unable to resist, I take my phone out and capture a photo for posterity. I don't even realize that I've started singing along with them until Sebastian comes forward, crooning right into my face. With Michelle back on his shoulders and holding her left leg tight, he takes the phone out of my hand, comes behind me, and takes a selfie of the three of us blaring to Bon Jovi.

With a fleeting glance at Claudia, I notice that she fetched her phone at some point and directs it at us. She looks blithesome, staring at the screen, probably videotaping our performance.

When the song ends, and everyone puts their cell phones away, Sebastian slides Michelle down from his shoulders and sets her on the counter once more. "I want you to meet someone," he tells her, leaning down as he points a finger at me. "This is Raff. He's my friend. He would like to say hello to you."

Michelle tears her infatuated gaze from her uncle and turns her head to me, really noticing me for the first time. And then her eyes slowly grow wide, and she shuts her mouth, losing her grin entirely. My heart stops beating briefly at her look, and I swallow. This was not quite the reaction I hoped for. The other two in the kitchen certainly didn't expect it either.

"Hey, baby doll, you all right?" Sebastian asks, his dark eyebrows drawn into a skeptical V.

The toddler lets go of him and brings her tiny hands close to her chest, clasping her fingers. Her every movement is slow as if her mind and body are in two different places.

"Don't worry, she's just a little shy with strangers," Claudia tells me, but from the sound of it, she's not entirely convinced that's the reason for the girl's reaction.

Michelle doesn't appear scared of me, really. Heck,

I don't know what exactly she *does* look like, but her gaze is so intense that it makes me uncomfortable.

A peace offering seems like the most diplomatic way to get through this, so I grab the pacifier I washed earlier and hold it out to her. In slow-motion, Michelle reaches out and accepts it, then brings it to her mouth, plugging it in. Her eyes never leave mine.

"Michelle?" Sebastian breaks through our weird moment. "Shall we show Raffael the rest of the house?"

I'm thankful that she nods and stretches her little arms toward him to pick her up. She presses her cheek to his chest as he carries her, but her gaze is still ominously locked on me.

Holding the girl with one arm, Sebastian bends quickly and grabs his duffle bag from the floor. "Bring your backpack," he tells me. "Our room is upstairs."

Room. Singular. He said *our* room *is* upstairs. Does he mean only one? The back of my neck begins to bristle. The house looks huge, they surely have a guestroom. Or I could just sleep on the couch.

Because Claudia follows us to the rear of the ground level after I fetch my backpack, I keep my mouth shut and my discomfort to myself for now.

A peach-tiled bathroom, the master bedroom, and Michelle's nursery are down the hallway behind the kitchen. The little girl's room looks straight out of a *Peter Pan* movie with a pink-upholstered seating bench beneath three beautiful bay windows, a cozy toddler bed with flowered sheets, a fort built of toy blocks in one corner, and a zoo of stuffed animals in another. The white-stained shelves and chests create a contrast to the dusky pink carpet and hold countless picture books and other toys. But the one thing that stands out is the white rocking unicorn in the middle of the room.

Claudia takes Michelle out of Sebastian's arms and carries her to the baby changing unit at the foot of the bed. "You finish the tour. I'll get the lady dressed in the meantime," she tells us over her shoulder. When she puts Michelle on the table and opens the zipper of her romper at the back, the little one's gaze stays fixed on me. It's as if she thinks I came from another universe and might disappear if she looks away for even one short moment. I give her a little wave and almost feel sorry for leaving her behind.

Sebastian takes me upstairs next, and we head to the room at the end of the short hallway. On the way, he quickly raps on three other doors, announcing, "Bathroom. Office. Claudia's former bedroom that's now just a storage room." Then he opens the last door and lets me walk in first. "And this is my place."

Reluctantly, I step into the surprisingly youthful room. A whiff of fresh bed linen lingers in the air, paired with the smell of the trees from the backyard. Blue curtains waft in and out of the open window above the light gray desk on the wall adjacent to it. To the left, a queen-size bed is centered against the wall.

I glance at the *Transformers* poster on the wardrobe door and then turn to Sebastian with a grin. "When did you move out of here again?"

"I was too busy screwing around with boys to invest time on renovations or redecorating." He sticks out his tongue at me, the immature gesture totally fitting with the style of the room.

Laughing, I lower to his bed and continue scrutinizing the place. The backpack slides from my shoulder to the floor. "Now I wonder what your apartment in London really looks like."

"Be nice, and I'll show you when we go home tomorrow."

My gaze locks with Sebastian's. An invitation to his home? The thought makes me smile.

"Come on." He nods at the door. "Let's see if the girls are ready."

I push myself up from the bed and walk out before him. Sebastian closes the door behind us.

"Your niece is really adorable." A grin overtakes my lips. "If you were the same kind of cute baby doll, I can see why no one had the heart to drown you in the sea."

For revenge, Sebastian pinches my ass. Hard. I give him a low, playful growl over my shoulder. Then my eyes instantly narrow, and I stop dead in my tracks. Damn. Did I really just moan with pleasure because he groped me?

Noticing my immediate discomfort, a slight frown replaces Sebastian's smirk. He grabs my chin and makes me look straight into his eyes. He's so close that I can make out the dark specks in his chestnut irises. "Don't overthink it, Raff." His voice is a soft command. "We're here because nobody knows you in this town. You can, for once in your life, be who you want to be without fear of what the neighbors will say." The skeptical lines in his face soften again as his hand slides to the back of my neck. "Let Eastbourne be your Wonderland."

I blink twice while his words slowly sink in. He's got a point. Whatever happens here doesn't have to affect my life back in London. I could...test. Play. Explore... Just be with Sebastian in a way that has felt good from the very beginning.

He skims the tip of his nose across my cheekbone and then groans in my ear. "And I really, really love it when you let yourself go."

The truth is, I love it, too.

Staring into his eyes again, I breathe in his warm scent. Then I nod. My personal Wonderland. I like the idea.

Sebastian gives me a smile that touches my heart because I think he's anticipating what's to come this weekend. I feel those ladybugs on my skin again, and this time, some butterflies in my stomach join the party.

CHAPTER 7

Raffael

Sebastian lopes down the stairs, and I follow him back into Michelle's nursery. While we were in his room, the sleepy toddler turned into a lovely princess wearing a red summer dress. She sits patiently on the baby changing table while her mother combs her thin, honey-blond hair. With her hands folded in front of her chest, she gazes at the door where Sebastian and I stand. She still has that otherworldly look in her sapphire eyes.

"Honestly, what did you do to my daughter, Raffael?" Claudia says and laughs as she notices we're back. "Brushing her hair is usually the worst torture in the world for her. We never get this done without a fit. And here she sits, as quiet as a mouse, waiting until it's over." She puts the brush away and instead grabs a wet facecloth from the table. Michelle closes her eyes as Claudia wipes it over her face once, from her forehead to her chin.

"She wants to be pretty for her prince," Sebastian teases.

I find it truly hard to look away when the girl captures me with her gaze. "And pretty she is," I say with a smile as I slowly walk toward her.

"I'll be out in the garden for a minute," Sebastian informs us and then disappears. To have a smoke while the girl is still inside, I imagine.

Claudia slips Michelle's left foot into a neat white sandal. I take the other one and buckle the shoe around her ankle. "Where's her dad?" I ask Claudia, curious because nobody said anything about when he'd be home.

With a frown, Claudia puts the romper that Michelle wore earlier in the hamper. "Her dad screws an English teacher in France now," she murmurs low enough so only I can hear.

"Ouch." I grimace.

"He left before Michelle was even born. We were only together for two years, and luckily not married." Claudia rolls her eyes and laughs bitterly. "He hasn't seen his daughter once since she was born."

That's a double ouch. How could one not want to see this little precious? Or be her daddy? Since the subject obviously presses on Claudia's mood, I drop it and stroke my fingers through Michelle's bangs. Then I carefully hold out both hands, ready to lift her down from the table, waiting curiously for her reaction.

Every time Michelle blinks, the sun catches on those blue gems and makes them sparkle. No smile, no laugh, just an incredibly intense look. And then she stretches her arms toward me; apparently, the sign that I'm now allowed to carry her.

Her arms folded over her chest, Claudia stands nearby and shakes her head, chuckling. "She's totally under your spell."

The feeling is mutual. Carefully, I take the child into my arms. When her big eyes are near mine, I smile and say, "Hi." No word slips out. All she does is look, blink, and breathe. "Wanna go out and find your uncle in the garden?"

She nods, and it's interesting to see that she at least reacts to my questions. When I put her down, she leads the way outside, but in three-second intervals, she turns her head over her shoulder to make sure I'm right behind her.

Sebastian leans against the huge tree in the front yard, taking the last pull of his cigarette. The moment Michelle sees him, she climbs down the front steps and runs toward him. Blowing out the column of smoke from the corner of his mouth, Sebastian hunkers down and swipes the cigarette on the grass. Putting it out, he then flicks the butt across the street so he can have his hands free for the girl. He lifts her up onto his shoulders again—obviously her favorite place.

"Guys, can I leave Michelle with you for a while?" Claudia asks from the doorstep. "I need to do the laundry and then start preparing everything for dinner."

"Sure. Can we take her to the playground?" Sebastian replies. "I'd like to show Raffael around town."

With the green light from Claudia, we head out through the small picket fence and amble down the street.

The houses in the neighborhood are enchanting, each with a neat front yard and painted in different colors: light blue, yellow, peach, purple. When I turn around at the end of the road and look back at them, it's like we're standing at the end of a rainbow.

Three kids play hide and seek in one of the gardens, and across the street, an old man with a white beard and no t-shirt starts mowing his lawn.

At the noise, I turn around so we can go on because I don't want Michelle to get scared by the sound. But she's resting her cheek on the top of Sebastian's head, her arms wrapped around his forehead, looking utterly happy—down at me. I don't think the lawnmower really bothers her.

Sebastian holds her left leg with one hand and points down the street on the other side. "I had my very first street fight right over there," he says proudly. "I think I was about eight years old."

"Wow." I laugh. "That's early to start fighting."

I've never been in a fight so far. "What was it about?"

He drops his arm as we slowly stroll on, and the back of his hand brushes against mine. "A little girl who couldn't walk without help lived in that house. Something was wrong with her legs, and she had to wear these splints on her knees. A couple of boys—maybe two or three years older than me—always picked on her when they walked by after school."

I squint against the sun. "You took on two at once?" My intrigued gaze wanders to his eyes, and again, I feel the brush of his hand against the back of mine. The caress is slower this time as if it weren't entirely unintentional.

"Yeah. I knocked one out cold with a stone to his forehead. Then I jumped on the other, and we battled on the sidewalk until Mr. Cooper, the girl's father, came out and yanked us apart."

I know that he walks deliberately closer now because there's only half an inch of space separating his fingers and mine. My heart starts beating faster at the thought that I could simply reach out and take his hand. I *want* to. Every damn cell in me does. But,

Jesus Christ, how can I?

"Even though I got the scolding of my life from my parents later," Sebastian continues and grins, "it was absolutely worth it. From that day on, neither of the guys badgered her again. And I was the little girl's hero."

He's become my hero, too. In so many ways. He's made me see things about myself. Understand them. Hate them. Love them. He didn't give up on me, even when I gave up on myself. And, somehow, I have a feeling that he never will.

At the next brush of skin against skin, my throat dries out. I want to shout at him for doing this to me instead of just taking my hand when it's so easy for him. I know why he doesn't, though. Why he wants me to build that bridge on my own. But every time I think I'm brave enough, something akin to an electric shock keeps my arm stiff, and my fingers tingling, aching for a touch I don't dare risk. It's so frustrating.

My chest heaves dramatically. A jump from a cliff would likely be easier than this.

"You're overthinking things again, Raff..."

Sebastian says in a soft voice next to me. Of course, he would notice my panic. He always does.

I close my eyes in the hopes of finding my center again. To calm my racing heart when Sebastian gives me no reason to be scared of anything. I wish I could be as brave as he is. I know it's possible. He keeps showing me time and time again that it is.

And then I stop giving a shit about any and all conventions in my life for once and move my little finger. This is my Wonderland, after all. Right? Here, where miracles can happen.

Tentatively, I stroke Sebastian's pinky and, from the corner of my eye, I see a tiny smile curving his lips. I hold my breath as time freezes at the end of the rainbow. It feels like a free-fall—not from a cliff, but from the very sky. It's so fucking scary, and yet exhilarating. But I know Sebastian won't let me plummet to the earth. He hooks his finger around mine and pushes my heart over the crest of this roller coaster ride.

This is it.

This is how I want to walk with him.

This is who I want to be.

Cautiously, I stretch out my index finger, too, finding his and hooking them in the same way, with our hands back to back. It feels as if he's pulling me home by just holding me. I never want to leave Wonderland again.

"What happened with the girl?" I break the silence after some time, my voice husky from the sensations flooding me in waves.

"Her family moved away a couple of years later. I never saw her again."

"That's really sad."

"Nah, it's okay. The couple who moved into the house after them had a son. Peter. He was my first boyfriend."

I roll my eyes and tilt my head back as I chuckle. "Of course. What else could it be?"

Sebastian grins and shrugs one shoulder, making Michelle's leg twitch.

We cross the street and take the road toward the beach that, according to a sign, is only five-hundred meters away. "You know," I tell him when we're back on the sidewalk. "I actually expected to meet your mom and dad here."

He remains silent for a moment and then glances at me. "My mom and dad passed away."

Oh. Wow. I don't know what to say.

"It's okay, don't feel bad," he tells me, giving me that soft, insistent look that I always get when he reads me. "They died many years ago."

A man in a gray suit comes down the street, walking his golden retriever on a leash. I want to let go of Sebastian's hand to step aside and let them pass between us, but Sebastian doesn't let my fingers slide away. He hooks them tighter with his and yanks me toward him as if to make sure I know where I belong. I like it.

The dog and his owner pass us on the edge of the sidewalk, and neither of them even looks at us twice.

"I was only thirteen then. Claudia was twenty-one," Sebastian continues, not feeling interrupted by the dog and his master.

"Did she care for you after their deaths?"

"Yes. She sort of raised me as her own child." He starts to grin. "So, whatever shit became of me, you can blame it on her."

I cast him a censuring glare, and he laughs. "No,

she did a great job, really. She's a good big sister. And an even better mom." At that cue, he lets go of my hand and takes Michelle down from his shoulders. We've reached a cute little playground with the endless sea as its backdrop. Sebastian sets Michelle on her feet near the entrance to the park and points at the baby slide. "Hey, look at that. Roger is here, too. You wanna go play with him?" Apparently, Michelle is supposed to know the toddler with his blue flap trousers, his hair so fair that he almost looks bald. Sebastian straightens and then waves at a pregnant woman sitting on a bench on the other side of the playground. "Hi, Laura," he shouts. "You know what it's going to be?"

The woman looks up from her book and blows her fringy brown hair off her forehead, greeting Sebastian with a smile. Her face wrinkles. "Twins! I don't care if it's boys or girls. They say it's gonna be freaking twins! I'm doomed."

Sebastian scrunches up his face in sympathy but laughs. In the meantime, I head to the empty bench close to the swing and sit down, gazing out at the ocean. Last time I saw the sea was two years ago in

Tenerife on vacation with Tanja and Felix. I love the rhythmic sound of the waves rolling to the shore.

Another sound—that of a toddler groaning as she struggles to climb onto the bench next to me—tears my attention away from the horizon. Startled, I watch Michelle take a seat on the bench, clasping her hands in front of her stomach, quietly looking at the ocean as I did before.

Sebastian stands a few feet away, his arms crossed over his chest. "Seriously?" he mutters, his mystified gaze focused on the two of us. "I'm starting to get a little jealous here."

"Don't be." I laugh and place an arm around the girl. "I'm just the new guy in town. They're always interesting. In truth, she only has eyes for you."

With a salacious gleam in his gaze, Sebastian comes forward, leans down, and grips the backrest of the bench behind me, caging me in. With his face close to mine, he drawls, "What if I didn't mean her?"

Cold and hot shivers run through my body. I wish I could grab him by his neck and haul him closer for a kiss. To show him who's got all my attention these days. Instead, I bite down on my bottom lip and blink. "Then you're lucky," I reply, somewhat hoarsely. "Because you've been on my mind 24/7 for a while now."

Sebastian waggles his eyebrows at me, pushing the corner of his mouth into a lopsided grin. Then he straightens and holds out his hand to Michelle. "If she doesn't want to play, we can go."

I stand up and take her other hand, lifting her down from the bench together with Sebastian. We stroll along the beach for a while, with Michelle between us until we take a path through the town and head back home. On the way, Sebastian shows me where he went to college, and we get the girl a strawberry ice cream cone. Most of the time, Sebastian has to lick the dripping cream from the side of the cone so her fingers don't get too sticky, but Michelle is happy with what she gets.

Once back home, we swing her into the garden, and then Sebastian tells her, "Quick. Run inside and tell your mummy to wash your hands."

Michelle hurtles off in a toddler-run that's heart-melting to watch.

I don't feel like going inside just yet, so I take a deep breath and soak in the golden afternoon sun. Feeling utterly happy and carefree for once, I amble to the mighty cedar in the front yard that sprouts thick branches in all directions. Some of them are low enough to reach with outstretched arms. With my back to the trunk, I hang on two of them and do a chin-up to test if they hold my weight.

Sebastian comes closer, and I lower myself again, leaving my hands on the branches. "Claudia and I climbed up there all the time when we were younger," he tells me.

Turning my head, I can see why. "This tree looks like every child's paradise."

"It is."

I face Sebastian again. He stands right in front of me now, lifting his arms to slide his hands over mine on the branches. His voice turns softer yet a little hoarse as he adds, "Some might also call it Wonderland."

I swallow.

The pressure on my fingers gets harder as he leans toward me. The pushed-back sleeves of his black hoodie reveal muscular, sinewy forearms. "So…" he rasps, his mouth getting ever closer to mine. "What will you do now, Raff?"

Once again hanging in the tree as I'd been tethered to the bedpost in my playroom before, I can't get away. But this time, I don't want to.

Holding his intense gaze, I breathe in the scent of his sun-warmed skin. The specks of black in his brown eyes mesmerize me, just as his barely-there smile does. And, somehow, I know that whenever I think of rainbows in the future, I'll always have the image of this very moment in my mind.

His chest pushes against mine, forcing my back against the trunk. Automatically, my breathing speeds up. I bet he can feel the beat of my racing heart reverberating through his ribcage. Mere inches separate us. Our lips. And yet, it's another torrential river that I need to build a bridge over. If only I knew how. Because I want to get to the other side…so damn badly.

Sebastian's breath strokes my skin as he softly whispers, "You're overthinking things again."

"I'm not."

"Then what are you waiting for?"

My gaze falls to his lips. "I don't know."

His fingers slide between mine on the branches. "Kiss me, Raffael."

And then, I do.

Just a touch of lips. I don't even have to move because he's right there. Closing my eyes, I let my mouth brush over his again. A firework display of shivers fizzles over my skin, covering my entire body. Every square inch of me is alert, alive in the places where he touches me, and also those he doesn't.

A rush of helplessness weakens my resolve as his tongue parts my lips. His firm hands over mine hold me steady, not allowing my body to escape him. He starts to circle my tongue with his in a thrilling game of lightning and thunder, touch and retreat. The warmth of his mouth sends tremors through me once again. Beneath the bite of his last cigarette, his tongue bears the sweetness of strawberry ice cream, and Sebastian lets me lick it all away. Slowly, tenderly, fervently. However I want.

The feeling of finally kissing him runs deep. It burns and tingles and strokes my insides with unimaginable pleasure. Sebastian's mouth on mine shifts my world off its axis and makes me float as if weightless—with him my only point of gravity.

In that moment when he softly moans against my lips, I realize that every kiss up to this point in my life was nothing compared to this. They were all meaningless. A barely-there breeze compared to the storm Sebastian ignites within me. With him, I catch a taste of Wonderland, and I know I'll never get enough of it.

His right hand slips from mine, and he gently brushes the strands of hair that always fall over my forehead and left eye to the side. His fingers move to the back of my neck, his thumb resting on my jaw as he deepens the kiss, holding me close.

My freed hand slips from the branch, and I slide my arm around him, clasping the hood of his sweatshirt at his back. Digging my fingers into the fabric, I cling to him with all that I have and all that I am as he kisses me on and on and on.

He moves his hand down my back, pulling me hard against him. With my eyes closed and my mouth meeting every kiss, I silently beg him to never let me go.

And he doesn't.

When the kiss comes to a slow end, leaving my lips wanting more, his arm is still around me, and he leans his forehead against mine. He pulls my hand down from the branch with his and then twists them so our palms are pressed together as our fingers intertwine.

I need a moment to catch my breath before I can look at him. His gaze is focused on me, only inches separating us. His eyes shine with hints of a smile even though it barely moves the corners of his mouth.

I never believed that it could feel so natural to be held by a man. Or to hold one back. I close my eyes again and savor the sensation of every inch of him pressed against me. My heart still races as if I've run a million miles to get here. And maybe I have. To come home. To find Wonderland.

"I'm so scared that it'll all end up in smoke the moment I let go of you," I croak into the small space between us.

"Well..." Sebastian squeezes my hand even tighter.

"Then don't let go," he whispers and catches my upper lip between his for a final, tender kiss. When his arm slides away from my back, our fingers are still laced, and that's how he pulls me away from the tree and toward the house.

This is the next hurdle I need to face. We won't be alone in there. A nervous tremor steals my breath. It's one thing to tell people that I'm attracted to men. It's an entirely different matter to face them head-on with a man attached to me.

The only thing I can imagine that would be worse is losing the feeling of Sebastian's hand holding mine. And so, I follow him into the kitchen where Claudia kneads a hunk of dough on the counter.

Her hands are covered in flour up to her elbows, and she smears some of it on her forehead as she wipes it with the back of her arm. Looking up at us, she asks, "Enjoy the walk?" She sounds a little out of breath from working the dough. Then she glances at our laced fingers.

For seconds on end, I don't dare move, not even when Sebastian changes the hand with which he holds mine and then loops his arms around me in an embrace from behind. I feel his strength at my back, supporting me, and still, my knees want to buckle and give out. My throat dries out, my tongue sticks to the roof of my mouth. And the entire time, my anxious gaze locks with Claudia's.

It's certainly not hard to read someone who turned into a terrified statue in the middle of your kitchen—sans breathing, heartbeat and all. Her sympathetic look doesn't waver from mine until her face splits into a heartwarming smile, and she tilts her head. "Don't be shy, Raffael. You two make a stunning couple."

As if she flipped a switch inside my chest with those words, my lungs expand and I'm able to drag in a noisy breath that I slowly let out through my nose. Sebastian starts to chuckle behind me, and Claudia laughs. I don't feel much like laughing. More like leaning across the kitchen island to hug her tightly.

The weird moment is interrupted by a small girl in a red dress, who comes through the door and holds out a book almost as big as she is. Glad for the distraction, I hunker down and reach for...the coloring book. "You want to draw a bit, princess?" I ask her, happy to have the full power of my voice again.

Michelle nods, her smile making her eyes gleam as if flooded with sunlight. There's a unicorn beneath a rainbow on the cover, and flowers sprout everywhere around the pink animal's legs. Obviously, someone has tried to repaint the bluebell flowers pink, even on the outside, and I can see myself facing my next challenge in this house.

Coloring with a two-year-old.

CHAPTER 8

It's homemade pizza for dinner tonight. While Claudia tops the first one with cheese, ham, and pineapple, I knead the dough for the other two and then roll them out to something at least close to a disc.

"So, he's finally opening up to you?" my sister asks in a low voice because Michelle has led Raff to the living room to color in her book.

"He tries," I murmur as I toss handfuls of grated cheese onto my pizza and then top it with salami and pepperoni. "I've never seen someone fight it so hard. But he's doing great." A smile slips. "You should have seen how carefully he touched my fingers earlier. It was heartrending."

My sister's hands still on the counter. After a couple of seconds, I lift my head because her penetrating stare makes me nervous. "What?"

When she smiles, her eyes bear the warmth of a midnight bonfire in the summer. Then she shakes her head and says, "Nothing. Just...do you know what Raffael likes on his pizza?"

That's not what she intended to say, and I know it. I'm positive something else burned on her tongue, but I don't press it. Especially since it's undoubtedly about me, and I'm not sure I like answering her questions. "No, but we can ask him." Wiping my hands on the dishtowel, I head to the arch in the wall and cast a glance into the living room.

Michelle sits on the couch, her legs angled so the soles of her feet are together. Braced on his left arm, Raffael lies sprawled across the rest of the L-shaped seat, his legs crossed and sticking out. Between them lies Michelle's favorite coloring book, the one I got her as a gift last Christmas. Together, they work on a page somewhere in the middle.

Both are concentrating so hard, I don't want to interrupt them just yet. Instead, I lean my shoulder against one side of the arch and watch them. When Michelle is done with whatever she colored dark blue, she holds out the crayon to Raff. He takes it without complaint and uses it instead of the yellow he was working with.

"They look so lovely together." Claudia's whisper drifts to me, and I find her standing next to me in the doorway. "Michelle is totally smitten by Raff."

I fold my arms over my chest and expel a quiet sigh. "Who wouldn't be?" There's still a hint of his taste on my tongue. A little bit of Sprite and a lot of just Raffael. He always tastes so sweet. I'm dying for my next dose of him to get me through the night.

A low ding chimes from Raffael's pocket, and he takes out his phone so gingerly that Michelle doesn't even notice. He reads, then swiftly types something and takes a picture of the open coloring book. After sending that to whoever wrote to him, he puts the phone away and continues with the blue crayon.

"Could you for once try not to go in like a bull at a gate with him?" Claudia begs me, placing her hand on my forearm. "He looks tough when on his own. But next to you, he seems almost fragile."

I realize I've been pretty tough on him these past two weeks. I didn't always need to be. And neither did I like to be. But with him, I face a wall so often, I didn't know how else to break through.

We overcame a big hurdle today. He lowered those walls. Entirely. And on his own, too. "I needed to use a little force to crack open his hard shell," I explain to my sister, still whispering as if it were the dead of the night and we were trying not to wake anyone in the house. "But I'll be gentle from now on."

With a quick sideways glance, I spot her happy expression. It's obvious that she likes him, and not just because her baby daughter is totally in love with him. Or I...

Just about to head back into the kitchen, she stops once more, her gaze fastened on the couch. Michelle stops coloring and puts her crayon down. Raffael doesn't notice because he concentrates on the page. Once again, the baby doll clasps her hands in front of her chest, utterly motionless as she stares at him. I haven't seen her this quiet since the day she got the rocking unicorn and didn't get down from it for almost three whole days.

All of a sudden, she stretches out her tiny arm and runs her fingers through the thatch of white blond hair that falls over Raffael's forehead. Surprised, he looks up, directly into her eyes. Neither of them moves or says anything for a fathomless moment. Until Michelle caresses him again and then leans her entire upper body forward to lay her head against his, closing her eyes.

At the flash from Claudia's cell phone, capturing the moment, Raffael's stranded gaze slides to us.

I cast him a smirk across the room. "She thinks you're a unicorn."

Helplessly, he quirks his eyebrows. *Absolutely edible, that guy.* Claudia takes another picture as he reaches out to cup Michelle's cheek and kisses her on the forehead. Then, she drags me back into the kitchen to finish dinner.

The last dough disk only has tomato sauce and cheese on it. I shout over my shoulder, "Hey, Iceland? What do you want on your pizza?"

"Anything is fine," he calls back, and then his words come from much closer. "Just no tuna, please." Carrying Michelle in his arms, he comes into the kitchen and stands beside me, scanning the bowls with the various toppings. "And no corn," he adds with a grimace.

I put a load on his pizza—ham, salami, peppers, a few pieces of pineapple and, after he sneaks a black olive from one of the bowls and pops it into his mouth, a handful of those, too. Claudia shoves all three pizzas into the oven, sandwiched on three baking sheets, and then decks out the table with four plates and cutlery.

Dinner only takes a few more minutes to start spreading a wonderful smell through the house. While we get the food out of the oven, Raffael places Michelle in her highchair at the head of the table and takes a seat next to her where I used to sit. We set the pizzas on everyone's plate, then I sit down next to Raff, and Claudia lowers herself into the seat across from him in her usual spot.

I wipe the Sprite can that I brought from the fridge with the hem of my hoodie and open it for

Raffael. No glass this time. I have a Coke for my meal and cut the pizza in eight slices, then I pull one out and lift it above my face to let the cheese drip into my mouth before I bite off the corner.

Raffael watches me, seeming unsure. I know that he likely wants to eat his pizza the same way now, but after a glimpse at my sister, who daintily cuts a slice of hers into small bites for Michelle, he grabs a knife and fork, too.

"Oh, no. Come on, snowflake! You don't!" Laughing, I turn to him and grab his hand with my free one to make him drop the fork. Then I hold out my own slice of pizza in front of his mouth, and he takes a bite because he has no choice. While he chews, I grab the back of his neck and pull him forward to press a quick kiss to his closed lips. "That's how you eat pizza in this house."

Immediately, he slides an uncomfortable glance to Claudia—for the kiss or for eating with his fingers, I'm not sure. He relaxes a little when she doesn't explode in a rant about either but just sends him a reassuring smile across the table and then bites off the tip of her own slice of pizza.

"See?" I laugh. "Everything's all right."

Well, almost. Claudia finishes cutting Michelle's dinner and offers her a small piece of cheesy pizza between her thumb and forefinger. The baby doll seals her lips and leans her head away. My sister and I stare at her in shared wonder. She has *never* refused pizza.

"What's up, sweetie pie?" Claudia asks. "There's only cheese on it, nothing else. You like cheese pizza." She tries to feed her again, but this time, the little one even squeezes her eyes shut and leans as far away as the chair allows to make her point.

It would be a hell of a lot easier to understand her if she said something—because she *can* speak. She's just been mute since the moment she caught sight of Raffael, and she got those huge hearts in her eyes. Which she still has now as she glances at him, looking hopeful and utterly in love.

"Somebody wants your pizza," I tease Raff and stuff the rest of my slice into my mouth, tearing the next one from the plate.

Not entirely convinced yet, he cocks his head and asks her, "Are you hungry?"

Michelle nods, and her shy smile lights up the room.

When he glances across the table, I assume Raff is considering taking a nugget from the plate Claudia prepared for Michelle. But he—as we all—knows better. Instead, he wipes the toppings from his own piece with a finger and then tears off a tiny bite, holding it out to Michelle. Her hands folded primly, she leans a little forward and opens her mouth, accepting with lovely gratitude the food he offers.

Claudia shakes her head, and we both laugh at them, then return to eating our own food.

"Careful, snowflake, or she'll take you to bed with her as her stuffed bunny, never letting you leave this town again," I say.

After he feeds her another bite, he turns to me with a grin. "Jealous, *Bash*?"

I hold out my slice of pizza to him again, and he leans forward to take a bite, not thinking.

Jealous?

No.

Happy I brought him to Wonderland?

Absolutely.

We stay sitting at the table long after dinner because every big sister in the world is curious about the person her brother hangs out with, and Claudia starts grilling Raff. Thankfully, about his ancestry and his architecture studies and not about his preferences in the playroom. It's a cozy and fun evening. We laugh a lot, and Michelle soon makes it clear that it's time to sit on the unicorn's lap instead of just admiring it from a distance.

When night falls, I leave the others alone for a few minutes and go outside to have a smoke. There was a time when I inhaled a whole pack within twenty-four hours, but over the last few months, I've reduced my cigarette consumption to only four or five a day.

I sit down on the front step of the house, my forearms braced on my bent knees, and watch the end of the cigarette gleam in the darkness. A silent click and light falling in a wide flood on the ground in front of me tells me that someone's coming out of the house. The door shuts again quietly, and the light disappears. Because the person doesn't come forward, I tilt my head just slightly, pressing my mouth against my shoulder.

Another moment passes before long legs clad in jeans walk past me in the darkness. I don't face Raffael immediately. I wait until he stops to stand in front of me. Slowly turning my head back, I take a deep drag from the cigarette and blow out a column of smoke, looking up at him. "Did she let go of you?" I ask with a quiet smile.

Raffael tucks his hands into his pockets. "Claudia's giving her a bath. But Michelle wants her Uncle Bash to read her a book later before she goes to sleep."

I nod and tease him, "Why? Doesn't she think that her newly adopted Uncle Raff can read?"

"Uncle Raff, sure. But unicorns...apparently not." He laughs softly. It's a sound that warms my insides. I like having these easy moments with him.

Through the smoke rising from the cigarette between us, I drink in his figure in the moonlight. There are moments I can't believe he's finally here with me. Looking back, the past two weeks have been a crazy roller coaster ride. Raffael is a snowflake. One that falls slowly, lands softly on your skin and, before you even know it, disappears again.

I can't even say when the initial attraction turned into real longing. The moment in the café a week ago when he told me that he doesn't like unpunctual people is a pretty good bet. His shy touches later that day were my downfall. And, even now, I love sending text messages back and forth with him.

The only thing that none of the above can top is the kiss we shared today. I've made out with a lot of people, boys and girls alike, since my years as a teenager. But in all that time, nothing has ever rocked my world as much as the moment when Raffael finally let me in. When he reached out to hold onto me with a shy need. It will forever be my undoing.

After kissing an angel, it's hard to imagine ever wanting anything else in your life.

I take the last pull of the Marlboro, snub it out, and then flick it away across the garden fence. Blowing out a lungful of thick smoke, I reach to the back of his thighs and drag him closer, spreading my legs so he can stand between them.

Mmm, maybe not such a good idea. His crotch at eye-level plants some dangerous images in my mind.

Michelle and Claudia are occupied in the bathroom. They won't come out for at least half an hour for sure. I let my flat palms run up the backs of Raff's thighs until they come to rest on his tight ass.

Snorting out an incredulous laugh, he smacks his hands over mine and pulls them away with more force than I've ever felt him use. "Don't you even *think* about it, Rhyse."

Damn, I like it when he dons the Dominant hat. And, heck, if that wasn't a challenge.

As soon as I get up from the front steps, Raffael's laughter ceases, and he retreats across the lawn. I'm pretty sure he wants me to follow him. With a low snarl, I prowl toward him and back him up against the tree.

His playful grin widens. "You wouldn't," he warns me.

Oh, if he doesn't misjudge me there. Entering Wonderland, I take his wrists and shackle them with my hands behind his back, locking gazes with him. "How are you going to stop me?"

Raffael laughs. Such a gorgeous sound. "I'll just scream. There's a girl in that house who loves me.

She'll come to my rescue."

Easing up on my grip of his wrists, I slide my hands down to lace our fingers and growl against his lips, "You don't want to be rescued." Then I claim his mouth in a hard kiss that knocks him back against the trunk of the tree.

Raffael feels like winter snow on my tongue. I could kiss him like this all night. And more...

Leaving his lips alone, I nibble a path down his neck, enjoying the tortured moan that escapes him. He wants me to stop, yet he doesn't at the same time. My hands move up over his butt, sliding beneath his hockey shirt and across his warm skin around to the front. But when my fingers hook in the waistband of his jeans, he grabs the branch above his head and pulls himself swiftly out of my reach.

With my head tilted back, I watch him climb up and quietly call out, "A blowjob in a tree is hard, but not impossible."

Raffael laughs as he settles himself on a thick branch and lets one leg dangle. "Get your mind out of the gutter and come up here."

Hoisting myself onto the first limb of the tree, I

follow his path up and sit on a branch next to him, leaning my back against the trunk the same way he does. From here, we have a perfect view of the moon and the million stars in the black sky. I haven't been up here in years. It's nice to be back.

One leg bent, foot resting on the bough, Raffael laces his fingers over his stomach and dreamily gazes out into the void. I watch him for several long minutes, memorizing every little detail of his face and etching this moment to memory. Only when I know I won't ever forget how he looks up here in the tree, I quietly ask, "What's on your mind?"

Another moment passes before he rolls his head to the side and slowly blinks. "A lot of things...about you and me."

Like a cigarette through parchment, his longing gaze burns into me. After some time, I swallow and reach out to him. Reluctantly, Raffael lays his hand in mine, and I close my fingers around his tightly. There's a barely visible smile on his lips, but the expression is most apparent in his blue eyes. He squeezes, too, then tilts his head back to look at the moon and the stars again. We both do. Together.

CHAPTER 9

Raffael

Sebastian climbed down the tree and went inside a few minutes ago after Michelle appeared in the doorway, holding out the book she wanted him to read.

Still gazing at the night sky, I try to sort through my thoughts. From the first day Sebastian walked into my life, he's wreaked havoc with my feelings. He still does. He bulldozes through my walls with such determination that I can't gather up all the brick stones fast enough to rebuild the barriers. And here I stand with a load of bricks in my arms, totally clueless for what to do with them. A deep sigh escapes me as my imaginary self lets them tumble to the floor. What a mess.

What a beautiful, scary, exhilarating mess.

I wonder if the mad carousel I'm on of realizing that I'm falling in love with a man will ever stop—or turn into something that feels at least semi-normal.

Right now, it renders me breathless.

I close my eyes for a minute, replaying the events of today in my mind one last time. It was an amazing day, and I wish it didn't have to end.

Then again, there are still a few hours left. Even though I'm a bit nervous about what the night with Sebastian will bring, a smile tugs at my lips.

I make my way down the tree and head inside, following Sebastian's voice to the back of the house. He's propped on the bed in Michelle's room with a book in his hands and the girl lying relaxed on his chest.

My hands tucked into my pockets, I lean against the doorjamb and listen to the story of Pinocchio running away from home. Michelle sees me soon enough. She doesn't move from Sebastian, her small hand clawed in his black hoodie, but her eyes stay glued to mine for several minutes. Until her lids slowly start to lower, and the sucking of her pacifier ceases to a twitch or two every once in a while.

Eventually, I cross to the bed, bend down, and breathe a kiss on her temple. "Sleep tight, little princess." I caress her hair, still damp from her bath, and then straighten, cutting a glance at Sebastian. "I'll take a shower."

He nods, and I leave the two of them alone so they can finish their bedtime story.

Claudia sits with her laptop in the living room, and I call out "goodnight" to her, too, before I ascend the stairs to Sebastian's room to grab my backpack.

The bathroom isn't as large as the one downstairs, and there isn't a tub up here, but it's light and friendly with the white tiles and cupboards made of birch wood. I strip naked and step into the stall, using my own shower gel to lather up. The warm water does wonders to refresh me after my limbs turned a little stiff in the tree. Since Sebastian is busy with the baby, there's no need to hurry, but I don't want to use up all their warm water either, so I keep it to ten minutes. After I've rubbed myself dry, I hang the used bath towel over the rack and then slip on fresh boxers and my jeans.

Barefoot, I sneak back to Sebastian's room and briefly halt at the door, surprised when I find the small lamp on the chest of drawers switched on, and Sebastian sprawled across the bed. With the pillow propped against the headboard, he has one arm angled behind his head, and his long legs stretched out and stacked. His eyes follow me through the room as I close the door and put my backpack on the desk. I thought I'd have a few minutes to myself after my shower. Finding that I don't makes my heart pound in panic. As I turn to the bed, Sebastian lays his free hand on the empty space beside him like an invitation. Rooted to the spot, I swallow.

"Scared?" he asks gently without so much as a sign in his face that gives his thoughts away. I start chewing on my bottom lip, which coaxes a smirk from him. "The room for baby girls is downstairs."

"Ha. Ha." Rolling my eyes, I cross to the empty side of the bed and slump down next to him, making the mattress wobble. Very much like him, I lean against the headboard, but with my arms folded over my naked chest.

"You don't have to be afraid. I won't bite. Promise," Sebastian teases with a wicked gleam in his eyes. Then he waggles his brows and drawls, "Unless you want me to."

With a cynical edge to my voice, I retort, "My ass still bears your bite marks from last weekend, thanks."

"Aaaw, come on. That was just a little nibbling." Abruptly, he leans over, startling me as he shapes his palm to my neck and hauls me closer. "And I know you liked it." His lips and tongue tickle my ear so unexpectedly that it sends shivers from the nape of my neck down to my toes.

Chuckling, I lower my chin in reflex to escape the sensation.

"What...?" he says with a playful tone and narrowed eyes as he leans away from me. "Shy again?"

Instant heat zings through my cheeks but ceases just as fast. I'm not, really. Okay, maybe a little bit.

"If you're still so frightened of touching a man,"

Sebastian teases, stretching to reach into the drawer of the chest at his other side, "you can draw your own map to go by on me." When he brings back a fat black Sharpie and grins at my face as he pulls up his hoodie to expose his hard stomach, I crack up laughing.

"You know you have a screw loose, right?"

He keeps smirking and takes his hand down, but I snatch the Sharpie from him before he can put it away.

"Give me that," I snap and roll to his side, swinging one leg over him to straddle his thighs. With wide eyes, he stares at me as I shove his sweatshirt up to his chest, then uncap the Sharpie with my teeth and spit the cap onto my pillow. It's actually a nice feeling to turn the tables for once and surprise *him.* I can see why he likes rendering me speechless so much.

"Hold that," I command, and he reluctantly replaces my hand on his hoodie. With my hand free, I brace my forearm on the mattress and get closer to my human canvas. Right where his black Maori tattoos end on his chest, I set the Sharpie on his skin.

At the first move of the felted tip along the valley between his muscles, his stomach quivers. Sebastian sucks in a sharp breath through his teeth.

"Tickles, huh?" I taunt him, looking up at his face.

He's still tongue-tied as his eyes hold mine with curiosity. I begin to draw a random pattern that seamlessly continues the ink on his pecs. Thick spirals in both directions, triangles with stripes inside, a double helix. To get more comfortable when I find it actually fascinating to draw on his skin, I shift and trap his right leg beneath my thigh. He bends the other one, his knee casting a shadow over my workspace. I hate drawing in the dark, so I push that leg to the side and earn a low growl from Sebastian. It's sexy as hell, but I refuse to give in to the urge to look at his face again. I just bite my lip instead.

So close to his body, I notice how his chest rises a little faster with his breaths at the beginning. I also see when it relaxes as the minutes tick by. But not once does the feeling of his intense gaze boring into me stop.

There're a few things about him I've been

wondering for a while, and since we're all alone now and have plenty of time, I take the chance to ask. "Did you always know that you were into boys and not just girls?"

His muscles tighten for a moment when he clears his throat. "I figured it out pretty early. Around eleven or twelve, I think. But I didn't tell anyone until I was sixteen."

"Was that when your neighbor down the road became your boyfriend?"

"Peter. Mm-hmm. Although we weren't together that long."

I quickly look up. I don't even have to ask the next question out loud, he just answers. "Two months and three days." Then he laughs. "He dumped me for an older guy at school."

Focusing on the tip of the Sharpie again, I murmur, "How long was your longest relationship?"

"With a boy or a girl?"

I give a nonchalant shrug with one shoulder, though I'd rather hear the details about his relationships with guys.

A sigh flattens his chest. "After Peter, I only had a

couple of girlfriends at school. And one at college. Nothing too serious. We only lasted for a few weeks because that was never really fulfilling."

"Fulfilling...?" I murmur.

"Yeah." A relaxed smile resonates in his voice now. "I soon figured out that I kind of enjoyed screwing around with girls, but the real excitement came with guys only." There's a short pause when he gets more serious again. "I think you can relate...right?"

My throat dries out, and the nape of my neck begins to bristle with a traitorous heat. I don't even dare to nod, but I believe my silence is answer enough for him.

"How long was *your* longest relationship with a girl?" He turns the tables on me, sounding really curious but hesitant.

My answer is clipped and honest. "I don't do relationships."

That puts an end to the conversation about boys and girls, fucking and love. For the longest time, there's only the sound of our breaths in the room. It's uncomfortable as hell.

"So...the *Transformers*?" I break the hush after a while with my totally random question, remembering the poster on his wardrobe.

"We all have our weak times," he says with an easy smile. I guess he's happy about the new subject, too.

"Which of them was your favorite?"

"Bumblebee," he tells me, and then we both chuckle, simultaneously blurting, "Of course."

In accordance with his fave movie, I draw a line of seven black bars next, each of them only one centimeter wide with the same amount of pure skin between them. A special bumblebee design.

When I run out of ideas for what to do next, I start on a very Celtic version of the letter S that winds up on the bar of the letter R. When his fingers suddenly skim across my forehead, slowly brushing my hair aside, I startle so hard that my hand jerks on his stomach. With regret, I notice that a blip now ruins the perfect design. "This is a Sharpie. Nothing can erase that for the next five days or so..."

From his guilty gaze, I don't think he intended to interrupt me. "I don't mind," he says quietly. When he trails his thumb down the bridge of my nose and then across my cheekbone beneath my left eye, my grief fades to complete oblivion. Hell. Is he trying to distract me?

His fingers are so much softer than the rest of him looks. Lowering my lids, I try to trace his movements with my eyes, but in the end, I just end up staring at his face again. The air begins to sizzle between us, and suddenly, all I can see is his lush lips. Lips I want to kiss.

But I don't. I'm not done with him yet.

Pressing my mouth into a reprimanding line, I cautiously move his hand away from my face. "You're not supposed to disturb an artist at work," I scold him, knowing full well that I'm stalling for time. And he probably knows it, too. But I don't care.

Every now and then, I have to scoot a few inches lower to keep drawing. My right forearm now rests in his groin because there's no other place for it where I have the right angle. Soon, a bulge starts to form in Sebastian's shorts. I force myself to ignore it and instead concentrate on my artwork. Next comes a very abstract rendition of a sea turtle, surrounded by ocean waves.

"Who did you send the picture of the coloring book to earlier?" Sebastian wants to know after a while when it's gotten really quiet in the room again. His voice sounds a lot huskier than it did five minutes ago.

"Tanja," I tell him, looking up at his face. He's pressing his head into the pillow, biting his bottom lip. Someone's trying to keep their control. I move my arm down a bit lower so my wrist lies directly on his cock. He closes his eyes. And I smile. "She'll be proud of me. I colored a squirrel blue today," I say, well aware of his pain as I keep drawing.

The unique Maori tattoo runs in a five-inch path from the right side of his chest diagonally across his stomach, passing just above his belly button. The waistband of his shorts stops me, so I drag it down just a tiny bit to finish the line of diamonds that functions like a frame to the pattern.

His breathing becomes irregular again. "Raffael..." he rasps.

"Hmm?"

That thing inside his pants, as hard as it is, really must hurt. I remember a night when I felt pretty much the same, being forbidden to come. With a sneer, I move higher again, resting my thigh on the very spot where my wrist was moments ago, and start to fill in the empty space beneath his heart, using a lot of black this time.

He croaks a throaty laugh. "You're doing this for revenge, aren't you?"

"Oh, you bet. For so many things..." I drawl scornfully, leaving lines of skin untouched that look like flashes in the night against the black. Or like the branches of a tree, with a crescent moon in the background...

After connecting the new drawing to the others in a sort of Y-shape, I take mercy on him and cap the Sharpie. Probably scared I might change my mind, Sebastian holds my wrist with one hand and takes the pen away from me with the other. Slowly. Almost tenderly. He puts it on the chest beside the bed then cups my chin, making me look straight into his fiery eyes.

Clearly, we're done drawing for tonight.

CHAPTER 10

Raffael

A tangible sizzle starts in the room, stroking over the bare skin of my upper body. The shivers run deep, all centering in my lower belly. Slowly, I push myself up from the mattress where I lay half sprawled across Sebastian's leg for the past hour. With his hand under my chin, he leads me where he wants me. Right above him.

Only his gaze follows my movements, the rest of him lies entirely still.

With one knee between his thighs and the other beside his hip, I brace myself on my hands to the left and right of his shoulders and just stare down into his gleaming chestnut eyes. Like earlier, when he disturbed my drawing on his stomach, he reaches to my forehead and brushes away my hair. This time, I don't startle. No. I breathe in, deep and slow, and let the scent of rainbows fill my head.

His fingers skim to the back of my neck. His thumb brushes along my jaw as he gently pulls me down—but not all the way. An inch before his mouth, the light pressure of his fingers stops. I blink once. Twice. With the third, my lids remain lowered, my gaze falling to his mouth. I inhale deeply one last time and let a sigh escape through my nose. Then I capture his upper lip softly between mine. It's just a whisper of a kiss as I breathe on it, but when Sebastian shapes his mouth to mine, it rekindles a thrilling tickle inside me. Everywhere.

Inching back marginally, I open my eyes and find him watching me with curiosity, a silent craving in his expression that makes me want to do that again. When I lean down a second time and touch his mouth, the tender bow of his upper lip tempts me to explore, so I trail the line with the tip of my tongue. Sebastian gives me all the time I need, but before I can pull away, he opens his mouth a little and finds my tongue with his. Only the tips of them meet in the faintest touch, but it's enough to start a simmering heat soaring through my body.

I love the taste of him. Beneath the faint layer of minty toothpaste that takes away the bite of his last cigarette, he reminds me of adventure and untamed desire. Of freedom. Because this is Wonderland.

I give his tongue another lick, just a small one, then one more, a little deeper this time. Suddenly, the pressure of Sebastian's fingers on my neck gets firmer again, and so does our kiss until we're all tongues and lips and fast breathing. I bend my elbows to lower myself because I want to feel him everywhere. But, still somewhat insecure, I keep my weight braced on my hands.

"Raff..." Sebastian growls against my mouth. "I'm not a girl. You won't smash me if you relax." And with that, he wraps his other arm around me, pulling me down onto him with a force that knocks my elbows aside and the air out of my lungs. I barely have time to catch my breath because he rolls us over until I'm trapped beneath him, our lips still dueling in a game of mind-numbing passion.

Sebastian's hands wander over my naked upper body, leaving a tingle on my skin everywhere he touches me. I want to touch him, too, feel his body, his muscles, so I shove up the black hoodie and let my fingers brush his skin on the sides of his torso. He reaches to the back collar of the sweatshirt and pulls it over his head then flings it aside. The full glory of his Maori tattoos, updated with my own design, spread over his body, capturing my gaze.

Once again fascinated, I skim my fingers over the black ink, not so shy this time. They're incredibly gorgeous. Hung up on the adornments of his chest that look like spikes spearing into darkness, I shove my hands to his shoulder blades and hold him down to me to kiss the design. I brush my lips along one of the inked spikes and let my tongue follow. Hell. He tastes exactly how he smells...a mix of sun and musk and very much just Sebastian.

My hands roam to his front again, tracing the lines and ink further. As I'm lying on my back, Sebastian straightens to a kneeling position, his legs apart. Looking down at me, he lets me explore.

I stroke my fingers over his stomach and down the valleys between his muscles, always keeping to the drawings. Until I reach the end of them where they disappear beneath the thick fabric of his beige jeans shorts. Seeking help, my gaze wanders back up to his face where the look in his eyes encourages me. It silently tells me that anything I want to do is all right.

I suck my bottom lip between my teeth. Then I warily reach out to the button of his shorts and pop it. My fingers brush the tip of his hard-on, and out of the corner of my eye, I see how his face scrunches with held back desire. The sound as I reluctantly unzip his fly tears ominously through the silence. I hook my fingers into the waistband of his shorts and boxers and then push them both down to carefully free his sex.

A low moan of relief hisses past his teeth. Yeah, he's been suffering for quite a while in these shorts. As much as the thought of crossing this very last line scares me, it raises intrigue and a longing in me, too. A desire to explore beyond the borders of the inked playground of his skin.

I roll to the side, bracing myself on my elbow, and leave the other hand hooked in his shorts. It's strange, but after every little step I achieve, I feel the need to search his eyes for reassurance. Sebastian is calm like the surface of a quiet lake. By the quick, shallow breaths that rock his chest, however, there might be a fire burning inside him, too.

Tentatively, my fingers slide along the waistband of his shorts, closer to his erection. He presses his lips together, not breaking eye contact for a second. Only when my fingertips gently stroke over his length does he shut his lids and take a deep breath, his nostrils flaring.

Never in my life did I think I would one day do to another man what girls have done to me so many times before. My very first blowjob. The word alone gives me shivers—and not only from fear.

My fingers glide around the center of his bone-hard cock, closing around his length, and I swipe my thumb across the head, spreading the sleek liquid that beads from the tip. When I pull his erection a bit away from his stomach, a new pearl forms. Suddenly, I want to know what he tastes like. Not just his kisses and his skin, but all of him.

His abs twitch as I lean over, and my hair brushes his skin. The moment I leisurely drag my tongue over the tip of his cock, Sebastian arches his back to brace himself on his hands behind him. A trembling whine breaks free from his gorge.

It's beautiful.

I rub my tongue against the roof of my mouth and savor his slightly salty taste. Then I give his cock another long, slow lick, from one side to the other. His erection twitches in my hand as more blood pumps into it. Carefully, I place my lips on it, shove them farther to the back, and gently graze my teeth over his velvety skin. After, I circle the tip of his cock with my tongue in a tender caress.

"Oh... *God*..." Sebastian groans.

A smile breaks free across my face. Now I understand why girls love this so much—teasing, when all you want them to do is suck. It's exhilarating to have the power. Knowing you decide whether the other drowns in ultimate pleasure...or burns in unspeakable craving. I love the sound of Sebastian whining for more.

I grant him a short reprieve and suck him in deep and hard while my own groin pulses with growing need. But then I let go of his cock entirely and kiss a path up his body so I can rise to my knees. The truth is, I think I don't want him to come too fast.

Pressing my tongue to the side of his throat and tracing circles that make him moan to the ceiling, I dig my fingers into his back and drag them down between his shoulder blades, certainly leaving red streaks.

Sebastian shifts his weight to one arm and places the other hand on the side of my face. Guiding my head until my lips align with his, he leans farther back, pulling me with him. We become entangled in a mad kiss again as he reclines, stretching out his legs and then hooking one of them around mine. He rolls us around once more, his fingers getting busy with the button and fly of my jeans. The moment I lie on my back, he pulls them down along with my boxer briefs. I've never been stripped naked so fast.

Gripping my ankle hard, he trails a line of kisses and gentle bites along the inside of my leg, up and up and up. My cock throbs with the pain of anticipation. I tilt my head back, flattening my palms against the bedsheets. My entire body stiffens when I feel his warm breath on my groin. He shoves both his hands over mine, holding them tight as he runs his tongue in a slow lick from my balls up the length of my erection to the very tip.

"Fuck, you taste like heaven," he rasps as he breathes a kiss on my stomach and then takes my cock into his mouth. He begins working me in a rhythm that drenches my body in sweat, and I know I won't last long.

The physical feeling of having a man blowing you is pretty much the same as a woman. But to know *whose* lips are wrapped around my cock right now sends the most thrilling shivers of pleasure through my entire body. Heat runs up from my legs and centers in my gut. I want to moan. I want to claw my fingers into the sheets. I want to explode.

But Sebastian doesn't let me. As if he knows exactly how far he can take me without crossing that line, he stops at the last possible moment and leaves me dying after building me up so fast.

He moves his body close to mine and up, then

shifts me a little as he slides behind me. Instantly, I stiffen when the realization of what he wants to do next hits me.

"Don't panic," he whispers in my ear and then feathers soft kisses on my neck. His hand rests on my stomach, his fingers gently stroking just my skin. "We're not going to do anything that you don't want."

His erection slides along the crack of my behind. He's still wearing his unbuttoned shorts, and the fabric rubs against my thighs.

"I—I don't *know* if I want this," I reply truthfully, my gaze set on the dark night outside the window. The thought of getting popped in the ass scares me a little, but it intrigues me as much as the rest of this dangerous game does.

"Then we'll try it," he murmurs against my neck, moving his lips up to my ear. "And if you don't like it, we can stop anytime. You'll keep control tonight."

His soft promise reassures me enough to give a slow nod and then close my eyes. Sebastian presses a kiss to the spot behind my ear, then a cold emptiness replaces his body at my back as he climbs off the bed.

I drag myself up to the pillow, dropping my sweaty face onto it. In the darkened windowpane, I can make out Sebastian's silhouette discarding his shorts and then taking something from the top drawer of the chest. He disappears from the glass when he kneels on the bed again, the mattress sinking behind me from his weight.

A brief rip of paper sounds out, then Sebastian spits the corner of a condom wrapper in an arc over me onto the floor. The scrunched-up rest of the packet follows suit. While he takes a few seconds behind me to put the condom on, I try to breathe myself back into a state of calmness. I don't want to be afraid of this. I simply refuse to. Everything we've done up to now has been nothing but beautiful. He won't hurt me. And if I find it's really unpleasant, he said that we could stop.

I trust him.

Moments later, he places his hand on my calf and slowly runs it upward over my thigh to my hip as he settles behind me once more. I close my eyes and try to surrender to his touch instead of fearing the unknown. His warm kisses on my neck and spine ease my tension a little.

"I'll be gentle," he says in a very soft voice next to my ear and then turns my face a little up to him so he can kiss me hard on the mouth. He pushes his left arm between me and the mattress and then laces our fingers, both his arm and mine wrapped around me in a loving embrace. I like it when he holds me like this. The nearness. With his chest pressed flush to my back, I think I can actually hear his heart beating with mine.

His other hand strokes along my side to my hip and then loops around my cock. I was prepared for him to work himself out, not massage me into oblivion again. But his fingers are so deft that after two minutes, I can barely grasp a clear thought anymore. I notice that he starts to push his crotch hard against my butt, but fuck, I don't mind. Heat fills me everywhere. It's as if someone has set my body on fire. Whatever he's going to do now is fine with me. As long as he doesn't stop what he's doing, and lets me please, please come in his hand.

With my head tilted back as far as possible, we kiss wild and slow and deep and passionately. His fingers tighten around my hand. His other hand brings Christmas to my dick. And, suddenly, his cock dips between my butt cheeks.

Sebastian lets go of me for the briefest moment to position himself, and then he slides into me.

Whoa. Awkward.

My eyes snap wide open as my ass gets stretched like never before. Thanks to the lube he must have put on the condom, it all goes very smoothly and doesn't really hurt. Sebastian doesn't go in far either. Just the tip of his cock. But it's enough to make him moan and bite down hard on my earlobe. That pain is certainly graver than what he does to my behind when he starts rocking in a very gentle way. And, damn, his hand is back on my prick, too, finishing me off with a few skilled movements. I don't know what to concentrate on first.

Shit! Is this what it feels like when the Jabberwocky fucks the White Rabbit in Wonderland?

My climax is the most intense one I've ever had, and finally, a hoarse cry breaks out of me as I skeet. I don't give a damn where the glibber goes, most of it is caught between Sebastian's fingers anyway. And by the tortured sound of satisfaction he gives from behind me, he's following me right over the edge.

With my face turned into the pillow, I pant myself down from the amazing orgasm. I miss his warm body at my back when he gets off the bed to discard the condom and clean himself up, but I'm helluva glad that his cock is no longer in my ass. It was all right as long as I was distracted with other sensations, but now, in the calm after the storm, I think it would make me feel really odd.

"I'm not exactly sure if I want to do that again," I murmur, the pillow smothering my words.

Sebastian's chuckle sounds from across the room. Moments later, the mattress dips behind me, and his gentle, clean hand runs up my leg as his lips caress the sensitive spot behind my ear. "Any of it?" he drawls and then strokes my butt cheek. "Or just that part?"

I drag my face out of its hiding spot and turn around to face him. His hand comes to rest on my other hip. It feels nice there as he lies sprawled on the bed, his head supported by his other hand. "Nah, most of it was okay, actually," I tell him, clasping the pillow.

"Just...*okay?*" His big, brown eyes widen, and I answer that with a devilish grin. Sebastian smirks, too. He grabs a strand of my hair from my forehead and playfully tugs at it twice. Then he gets up again and smacks me hard on the ass.

Ow.

"Up with you and into the shower," he orders. "I still need a cup of coffee before getting back to bed."

Moaning, I roll off the mattress, grab my jeans, a t-shirt, and fresh boxers from my backpack, and follow him across the hallway.

CHAPTER 11

Sebastian

I step into the shower stall first and turn on the water. Raffael stretches out his hand to test the temperature before he dares to join me, which makes me chuckle. "Always such a scaredy-cat."

He sticks his tongue out at me then faces the spray of water, closing his eyes. It's cramped in here, nothing compared to the spacious shower he has in his apartment, but I like the nearness. To be honest, if I could, I'd have dragged him around with me everywhere in a tight hug. There were moments today when I just wanted to grab his face and kiss him hard, simply because he said something sweet or, once again, gave me one of those shy looks that I love so much.

The day with him was amazing. I'm glad Claudia suggested that I bring him with me on this trip. It was just what he needed to get all the shit of London out of his head. To dare to take the next step into another world. Into Wonderland.

I don't know many people in the city yet. Some guys in the fitness center and a few people from the racing community. None of which I would call a close friend. So, Claudia was the first person I told about the strange beginnings of my friendship with Raffael. And my feelings that grew for him. Fast. After our parents' deaths in a train accident, Claudia became more than a sister to me. She's my closest confidant. It makes me happy to see that she took to him from the moment he walked into the house. And the baby doll? Well, she would adopt him as her pet unicorn in an instant if she could.

Raffael runs his hands through his drenched hair, shoving it back with his chin tilted up. He has the most exquisite body I've ever put my fingers on. Strong and defined, yet somehow fragile in the way he moves. Lithesome, like a leopard. A *snow* leopard.

Only absently, I notice how his gaze switches to me through the downpour of water. He holds out his shower gel and nods at my stomach. "You want to wash that away?"

Slowly, I look down at myself—to where the real ink on my chest runs into the Sharpie drawings that bear both our initials. Get rid of this? No way in hell.

I know he was stalling at the time because he was nervous about being in the room with me alone. But the way he lay sprawled across my leg the entire time, the way he concentrated so passionately on the task of making the designs...I couldn't look away from him for even one second. Everything about the ink on my skin is perfect. Even the blip that happened when I made the mistake of touching him.

Or *especially* that blip.

Raff is always so jumpy when it comes to touches. And scared. It's the sweetest thing in the world. And I love him for working up the courage to get over that. Because he wants to be close to me, just as I want to be close to him. The warmth that rises within me at the many memories we made today is overwhelming. It clogs my throat and puts a feeling of longing for him in my chest that I can barely contain.

"I don't think it'll work with just soap and a sponge, though." His soft voice breaks into my thoughts. "You might have to use a coarse scrubbing brush."

"Raffael...?" I rasp, finding his gaze through the spray.

My hoarse voice triggers his anxiety. "Hmm?"

But we've said enough. I cup his cheeks, push him against the wall with my body, and claim his mouth in a kiss full of need, longing, love, and all the other things I can't name at the moment.

A tiny, surprised gasp escapes Raffael. It gets caught by the passion springing to life between our lips and twined tongues. His fingers dig into my back, and his clingy embrace makes my heart beat in a rhythm I've never known before. I don't want to let him go. Ever. Again...

So, when we break the kiss, and Raffael pants for air, I lean my brow against his and close my eyes.

"Is everything okay?" he asks warily, his right

hand resting lightly over my pounding heart.

I nod. That's all I can do.

Because everything is perfect.

CHAPTER 12

Raffael

Sebastian surprised me a little in the shower. Actually, he shocked me. I don't know what train of thought I ripped him from when I offered him my shower gel, but it was obviously a deep one.

With my jeans and a white t-shirt on again, I rub my hair dry, keeping an eye on Sebastian. He's dressed in blue jeans, too, after the shower and straightens his black hoodie over his stomach. The Sharpie drawings didn't lose any intensity under the water. They likely won't for another couple of days. I wasn't joking about the coarse scrub brush earlier. Permanent marker is hard to remove from skin.

We put the used towels in the laundry and head downstairs into the kitchen because Sebastian said he wants a cup of coffee before bed. I don't know anyone who drinks espresso at midnight, but then he's special in many ways. It's just another thing that adds up to the puzzle that makes him perfect for me.

Flaring light comes from the dark living room, causing us both to stop. Claudia has fallen asleep on the couch with the TV on. "Can you turn it off?" Sebastian whispers to me, already heading toward his sister. He scoops her up from the couch along with the crocheted blanket she's covered with and answers her incoherent murmur with a, "Time to go to bed, Clauds."

I look for the remote and find it in the space between the cushions. The room falls into utter darkness as I push the off button, so I follow the small light above the oven that Sebastian turned on in the kitchen. He comes back moments later and asks, "Do you want coffee, too? Or something else? Tea or hot chocolate?"

"Hot chocolate would be nice."

He nods and fills a mug with milk from the fridge,

then puts it into the microwave, letting it circle for a bit. In the meantime, I hoist myself up onto the kitchen island and then grimace because sitting after *that* kind of sex feels a little weird.

Sebastian chuckles at my awkward expression. "We don't need to do it again if you didn't like it." He puts a cup under the coffee machine. While black liquid pours into the mug, he takes my hot milk out of the microwave and enhances it with a generous splash of chocolate syrup. Placing the warm drink in my hands, he murmurs in my ear. "But it was nice to be your first."

I smile down at the cocoa I hold in my lap. "That means something to you, huh?" Honestly, I never got the hype of *first times*. Not in the past anyway. Inexperienced girls bothered me rather than got me excited. To be the inexperienced one now makes me feel a bit insecure.

With his knuckle under my chin, Sebastian tilts my face up. "It means everything," he tells me softly.

He's right. All the *first times* I had with him these past few weeks touched me, as well. And there were many of them. I couldn't decide which was my favorite, but stargazing in a tree and just holding hands with him ranks pretty high on the list. Right under the taste of strawberry ice cream and cigarettes on my tongue.

Sebastian gets his coffee and leans against the counter across from me, his ankles crossed and one hand on the edge of the worktop. He watches me over the rim of his cup as he drinks. I take a sip of my hot chocolate and lock gazes with him. I know he can see the smile that I'm hiding behind my mug.

"Don't," he says and puts his empty cup into the sink.

"What?"

When he comes forward, I lower my drink and automatically spread my legs so he can stand between them. With his hands braced on the countertop on either side of my hips, he stares intently into my eyes from the inches that separate us. "Don't hide. You're stunning, Raffael, especially when you're happy."

My fingers wrap tighter around the mug. How does he always make my skin rise in goosebumps with so few words?

"I want to spend more time with you. Not just here where nobody knows you. I want to be with you tomorrow. When we're back in London. Next week, next month..." He brushes his nose across my cheekbone. "Don't let it end in Wonderland."

My heart begins to pound really hard. I don't know where the sudden nervousness comes from, because I want to be with him, too—and not just tonight in Eastbourne. But thinking beyond the borders of this safe place makes me dizzy. Like there's a swarm of bees lodged in my head, and their dangerous buzzing prevents any rational thought.

"I—" My voice lets me down, so I clear my throat and try again. "I don't want it to. It's just that—"

"No. Don't find excuses now." He cuts me off and trails feather-light kisses along my neck.

I tilt my head a little to give him better access because it feels much too good.

"You don't have to tell the whole world that you're gay tonight," he murmurs against my skin. "Just stop hiding from yourself. And from me." His tongue swirls over the crook of my neck, sending exquisite little shivers down my spine. "Let's try a relationship."

A thousand thoughts try to get past the noise of the swarm of bees in my head. Images of him holding my hand in the street. Of getting picked up by him after a day at the university. Of introducing him to my family in Iceland. The cocoa cup begins to shake in my hands. "You want me to be your boyfriend?"

Sebastian's lips move up the side of my throat until he catches my earlobe between his teeth. "I want you to be my everything."

God, why does he always bring on such scary thoughts with the best feelings in the world? I want to surrender to him and make him stop talking at the same time.

But I want to be with him, too. And if the right name for it is *boyfriend,* then maybe that's what I want to be. Why is it just so hard to say it out loud?

"Jesus Christ." I moan and dip my forehead to his shoulder. "Crack can't be as bad as you."

The warm breath of his chuckle dampens my skin. "I love being your drug."

"No doubt," I grumble and slide off the counter,

moving him out of the way. Quietly, he watches me as I finish my hot chocolate and put the mug in the dishwasher. When I return to him, there's a curious furrow in his forehead that I decide to ignore. Instead, I just take his hand and pull him out of the kitchen.

"Does that mean *yes* now?" The playful smile in his voice is much too sweet and makes my heart melt.

But I keep a straight face. I don't turn around, just walk upstairs with him. "That means it's late. It's been a long day. I'm tired. I've been fucked in the ass. And I really need a couple hours of sleep before I can think about anything else."

Sebastian laughs behind me. "In my arms?" He lets me drag him every step of the way.

Shit, now I have to bite off my own grin. But it doesn't work so well. "Perhaps."

In his room, I let go of him, strip down to my boxers, and then belly-flop onto the bed, facing the window. Soon enough, the mattress shifts as he climbs in behind me. It doesn't escape me that he doesn't turn off the light immediately. And, heck, I can feel his irritated gaze on the back of my head. It makes me smile to myself.

"You aren't *really* going to sleep like that, are you?" he mutters after a couple of minutes. Finally, I do crack up laughing.

I turn around and find him clinging to the pillow he lies on, pouting like a little boy. "What?" I demand. "Too little body contact?" With a provocative smirk, I shove my knee forward to rest against his, just like he did when we were in the cinema, and I couldn't bring myself to touch him. "Is that better?"

"No." He doesn't break eye contact when he hooks his leg around mine and pulls it over to his side, leaving them tangled. Then he grins. "*Now* it is. A little."

It is, indeed.

We stare at each other, and I wait for him to turn off the light. He doesn't. "What do all the patterns on my stomach mean?" he asks.

Of course. Apparently, sleep is overrated. Then again, I like that he doesn't want to let the day end yet, so I prop up on my elbow and push at his shoulder to make him roll to his back. "This," I say and trace my fingertip along the double helix I drew at the beginning, "is for the weird characteristics that nature equips you with when you're born."

"Like being gay?" Sebastian asks, scooting up a little so he can look at the things I point out.

"Like having blond or black hair," I retort sarcastically.

"Ah, right." He rolls his eyes, and I chuckle. Then I move my finger to the bumblebee bars.

"This pays homage to your crazy love for weird comic movies in your youth." I waggle my brows at him. "It means: Bumblebee forever."

Laughing, he wipes the blond strands away from my forehead, but he takes his hand away again quickly. "You aren't really a *Transformers* fan, are you?"

"Well, I'm more a *Fast & Furious* type of guy."

He accepts that without comment. "So, what's the turtle for?"

I follow the lines of the abstract sea turtle's carapace. "It's for a lovely walk down by the ocean." My voice goes a bit softer. For a moment, my gaze lingers on the intertwined letters R and S. I refuse to explain what that stands for because I think, by now, he's figured out where all this is going. Instead, I move my finger to the more prominent theme beneath his heart.

Sebastian lays his hand over mine and traces the branches of clean skin against dark with his fingertip. "A tree against the night sky?" he asks softly.

"Wonderland..." I rasp.

His fingers close gingerly around mine, and he waits until I finally look up at him. "You captured *today* on me?"

For a few heartbeats, I'm a prisoner of his warm chestnut gaze, then I glance back at the drawings. My voice is barely a whisper as I tell him, "I think I captured *us* on you."

A hush falls over the room, and it almost makes me want to take back my words. A beep from the pocket of my jeans on the floor rescues me from the moment. I slip out of bed and retrieve my cell phone. This late at night, it can only be Tanja or Felix, and I've been waiting for this message all day. Sitting on the edge of the mattress, I smile as I read what Tanja has to say.

"Your friends?" Sebastian wants to know, sounding as if he's back from the sentimental plains of Wonderland, too.

I nod. "Felix finally let the cat out of the bag. And Tanja is freaking out a little right now." She complains in way too many words that I'm *never* in town when something important and crazy happens. Yeah, right. Because I'm running off with strangers like *every* weekend.

I push the pillow against the headboard and recline, slipping under the covers that Sebastian draws up. The heat of his legs warms the space quickly, and I like it.

Using both thumbs on the display, I type a message back to Tanja: *Calm down, baby. I don't know how we didn't see this coming, but it's all you want and need. Felix is the perfect fit for you. You know it. And I won't drop out of your life just because you have a boyfriend now, promise. I might have one myself sometime soon. :P So, put your big-girl-pants on and tell him the fuck YES. And if you're really too scared to take that jump, there's a coloring book in my apartment that you can borrow and paint yourself some courage with. ;-)*

I send off the text, happy about the sticky-tongue smiley and three hearts that she sends back straight away.

I want to put the phone away, but I don't get a chance to because Sebastian swipes it from my fingers. The complaint gets stuck in my throat when he holds the phone above his stomach and takes a picture of the pseudo-Maori ornaments.

He sends it to himself through WhatsApp, using the thread we've had running for two weeks, then he startles me as he loops his arm around my neck, yanks me closer, and holds my phone in the air to take a selfie. While he leans in to kiss me behind the ear, I drape my forearm over my eyes, unable to keep the smile from my face.

He sends that to himself, too, and my heart skips a beat when I catch a glimpse of it. It looks kind of sweet and hot and forbidden and totally insane all at the same time. Sebastian also types a few words afterward, but he closes the app and hands my phone back to me before I can read it. Curious by nature, I reopen the thread and then blurt out laughing.

Me

The first photo of us as a couple.

I write my own text to that and shoot it right back after the one he posted on my behalf.

Me

Yeah...no. You know that we aren't a couple.

Sebastian reads along as I punch in the words and then grabs my phone once more, correcting it the way he sees fit.

Me

...just yet. But we'll talk about the option when we're back in London.

Me

Maybe. Goodnight, Sebastian.

Me

Goodnight, Raff.

While Sebastian rolls to the edge of the bed and switches off the lamp on the chest of drawers, I roll to the other side and put the phone on the nightstand. Before I even have time to sink back into the pillow, his arm wraps around my middle, and he hauls me against him. A tiny gasp escapes me, then I laugh quietly as my head comes to rest on his outstretched arm.

He plants a kiss on my neck, and I close my eyes, breathing in the scent of rainbows in Wonderland.

*

My face and shoulders are pleasantly warm, like someone put my upper body in an oven, even though the blanket has slipped down to my waist. Lying on my front with my arms pushed under the pillow, I blink my eyes open, getting blinded by the sun flooding the room through the window. I must have slept through half the morning.

We.

Sebastian's arm is draped over the small of my back, his motionless fingertips loosely grazing my side.

"Good morning," he says softly behind me. It surprises me a little.

"How did you know I woke up?" Jeez, my voice is croaky.

His fingers start to caress the side of my stomach. "You breathe differently when you sleep."

"How long have you been listening to my breathing?"

"An hour or so."

Jerking up, I prop myself on my elbows, casting him a narrow-eyed glance. "Seriously?"

Sebastian laughs, rolling onto his back. He angles one arm behind his head. "You're a sound sleeper. One would probably have to tip a bucket of water over your head to wake you."

Only now I notice that he's actually dressed. Jeans and a black, ribbed tank top. When the hell did he get up? Easing my shoulders, I drop back onto the pillow, keeping my focus on his eyes.

"Are you hungry? Claudia and Michelle have been up for hours, but I can make us breakfast if you want," he offers.

"I don't eat breakfast. Just a cup of coffee is fine."

"Cappuccino with a shovel of sugar?" he teases and makes me smile. Then he swiftly gets up and slips into his dark red sneakers. By the door, he turns to me. "Come down when you're ready."

I heave a deep sigh, closing my eyes for another short moment after he's gone. Then I finally get up and slip into the clothes I wore after our midnight shower. After brushing my teeth, I head downstairs and follow the sound of voices into the kitchen. It's Sebastian, Claudia, and an elderly woman who seems to be new to Sebastian, too, because they're shaking hands.

When they see me coming, Claudia greets me with a warm smile, and holds out her arm, beckoning me closer. The woman with the short, graying curls and wrinkles that tell a story gives me a friendly once-over. "Another brother of yours?" she asks Claudia but extends her hand to me. I shake it.

"No. Raffael is a friend of the family," Claudia answers. Then she tells me, "This is Mrs. Shoemaker. She and her husband moved in across the street only a couple of months ago."

The shapely seventy to eighty-year-old woman in her simple white blouse and flowered skirt looks like anyone's grandmother. Her hand is warm, chubby, and soft. She holds a pack of flour in her other arm, so I guess she came here to borrow some ingredients to bake cookies for her grandchildren or something.

"Nice to meet you," I say, but my gaze soon drifts to Sebastian, who walks forward to hand me a cup of steaming coffee.

"With extra, extra sugar," he whispers as the women get caught up in a conversation I no longer pay attention to.

I accept the mug with a smile and take a sip. "Mmm, perfect. I think I'll keep you," I tease him quietly.

"As your barista?" Sebastian sticks out his tongue at me.

"If you can make good lasagna, too, I might upgrade you to my cook."

He waggles his brows in an insinuating way that gives me goosebumps. "So, you want me to cook dinner for us tonight?"

"That's not what I said." I roll my eyes but laugh

until I spot someone even sweeter than Sebastian over his shoulder. Michelle sits on the tiled floor in the living room, wearing a cute yellow dress with puffy sleeves. With the mug in my hands, I head over and hunker down in front of her. She doesn't immediately notice me as she tries to press a bunny-shaped wooden piece of puzzle into a recess that obviously requires the form of a dog.

"Good morning, little princess," I say in a soft voice, trying not to startle her. But her face snaps up to me anyway, her eyes lighting up with joy. She holds the bunny out to me, and I set it into the correct spot on her baby farm puzzle.

Then, something behind her catches my attention, and I slowly straighten again.

It's the news on TV. A woman in a red business dress faces the camera while video clips of yesterday's Gay Pride Parade flash on the screen behind her. The whole thing looks like a huge Brazilian carnival. I recognize Oxford Circus and Regent Street as the thousands of people party along, apparently having the time of their life.

The one thing that irritates me is the grave look

on the speaker's face.

"A shadow was cast over the event by the counter-demonstration outside town…"

New video clips broadcast. Skinheads in bomber jackets and combat boots march. They bellow and hold up signs on poles that read…really nasty things. My throat dries out, and I'm barely able to blink when the anchorwoman's words float into my world like an echo from far, far away. "…deserted factory…riots…two people brutally beaten…a homosexual couple…doused with petrol…"

My breathing comes to a complete stop as my horrified gaze fixes to the TV.

"Set on fire."

Blue light flashes on the screen. Paramedics push two stretchers into separate ambulances. The upper body of one victim is visible for only a second. Arms, torso, and head…burned.

I'm getting sick.

"…messages sprayed…"

Huge, black letters flash on the grimy wall of the factory behind them. My vision is a blur of white and black spots dancing into each other. I merely glimpse the words: *DEATH … HOMO PIGS … BURN!*

Whatever the anchor says next is lost to the sharp voice of the friendly old grandmother with the flour for her cookies behind me. "It's been all over the news this morning. If you ask me, it's their own fault. Why don't they stay home? Always have to have these stupid parades, exposing themselves like display dummies."

My tight throat barely allows me to swallow as I turn around on autopilot. The disgust in the nice granny's eyes bores into me like a thousand glowing lances.

"Herbert and I always say that the world will go to the dogs if those freaks are allowed to do whatever they want," she snaps. "And here's what we get."

What we get…? The attempted murder of two men guilty of nothing but loving each other…is what *we* get?

My gaze snaps to the pale faces of Claudia and Sebastian behind her. "Estelle—" Claudia gasps as she comes toward me.

I press a hand to my stomach as something in there wants to come back up. Claudia takes the cup out of my hand, and I let her, but I can't look at her. Sebastian is my only focus. The man who made me kiss him. Touch him. Whose cock I had *inside* me last night. An acrid burn travels up my throat. Images of me facing a group of skinheads flash in my mind. My eyes start to burn. I think I forgot to blink for nearly a minute. In my mind, I see them pouring gasoline over my body. Over Sebastian. Over every gay person in the world.

And they make us burn.

Because we *deserve* it.

Because we're *freaks.*

Because the friendly grandmother from next door said so.

"Raffael..." Sebastian rasps, rooted to the floor just as I am.

But I don't want to speak to him. I don't want to listen. I don't want to be here.

I don't want to be gay.

I need to get out!

CHAPTER 13

Sebastian

Raffael stares at me as if the mere ghost of him is standing in the living room while his body got burned outside London near the deserted factory last night.

I have no idea why this terrible, bigoted woman is still in our house, but I hope she'll one day get what *she* deserves for what she just said. For the horror-stricken look she put in Raffael's eyes.

If Claudia hadn't taken the coffee mug out of his hand, it likely would have shattered on the floor. "Raffael..." I whisper because I have a feeling that the last thing he wants me to do right now is walk over and hold him. And yet, I take a small step forward.

He cringes the moment I move, and then whirls around and storms out the door.

"*No! No! No!*" I shout, shoving the stout Mrs. Shoemaker out of the way as I dash after him.

Raffael doesn't get very far. In the shade of the cedar in the front garden, he braces one hand on the trunk while he presses the other to his gut and pants for air. I slow down and warily draw closer. "Raff…"

He looks up at me with sheer desperation, his pale face drenched in a cold sweat. "No—" The sharp word freezes me on the spot two steps away from him. He squeezes his eyes shut, his voice turning weaker. "Just…don't." And then his body convulses, and his stomach forcefully gives back the few sips of coffee he took earlier.

Helplessly standing aside, I can only watch with a constricted chest as Raffael falls to his knees where we kissed yesterday and throws up on Wonderland. My heart bleeds for him—for both of us.

Low murmurs behind me make me cast a glance over my shoulder. Mrs. Shoemaker comes out of the house, attended by my sister, who carries Michelle in her arms. The old woman gives me a mystified look as the truth of what's happening obviously sinks in. I glare back at her until she's past the garden fence, then I no longer give a shit and squat beside Raffael.

The moment I touch his shoulder, he flops to the side, sitting in the grass with his back jammed up against the tree. He pants fast, his gaze turned up to the clear blue sky.

"Hey," I say in the gentlest voice I can manage and grab his ankles to give my words more weight. "It's not true. Whatever that woman—"

"I want to go home." He cuts me off, still looking at the sky and not me.

"Listen, let's go inside and just—"

"No, Sebastian!" His scowl full of panic and rage zooms to me. "I want to go home. Now." When his look moves a little up to where Claudia stands with Michelle, judging by the shadow next to me, he closes his eyes in pained shame. He doesn't want them—or me—to see him like this.

I swallow hard, but it's clear that now isn't the right time to talk. He wants to leave, so that's what we'll do.

I rise from the ground and give Claudia an apologetic look, which she returns with sorrow in her eyes. It's nobody's fault, really, but everyone feels miserable. Even Michelle looks stricken for her beloved unicorn. I gently stroke her cheek. "Raffael doesn't feel well today. I'm going to take him home now."

She nods, but her baby face fills with sadness.

I run inside and get our things from my room, then I grab a water bottle from the fridge before I head out again. Raffael already waits by the Honda, his head lowered so he doesn't have to look at anyone.

Only when my sister walks up to him with the little one does he murmur a quiet, "I'm sorry."

Claudia lays her hand on his forearm. "Don't be," she tells him, but I doubt that he really hears what she says. I throw the luggage into the back seat and hand Raff the water before he gets into the car.

Since I don't want to let him wait too long, I give my sister a brief hug and promise to call her later. Michelle gets a loving kiss on her cheek. Then I slide behind the steering wheel, slam the door shut, buckle in, and start the engine.

With one last glance at Raffael, I hope to see that we can talk this out, but he just turns his head to the side and looks out the window as he takes a sip of water from the bottle. He's rebuilt all his walls—and fortified them. So, I back out of the parking spot and drive up the road.

The streets are empty this Sunday morning. Still, I don't speed. I don't know why. Perhaps because there's a small hope lodged in my chest that Raffael might come around and talk to me after a few minutes—ten, twenty, fifty, an hour. But his lips stay sealed.

The oppressive silence in the car is unbearable. I roll down the window to at least get some noise from the outside. I don't dare turn on the radio. The open window helps shit. Breathing doesn't get any easier because of it.

A scream of panic rises within me that this is it. Raff will never open his mouth in front of me again. We'll never touch the way we did last night. The happiness we just found has slipped through my fingers like the sand in an hourglass.

Casting a glance at him every now and then, it pains me to see how his chest still jerks with frightful pants. His throat twitches, and in the past half hour, he's sucked his bottom lip between his teeth more often than I've ever seen him do before.

As we cross the borders to London, the traffic increases slightly. Fortunately. Because it'll slow us down. I'm afraid to think of what will happen when we turn into Brook's Mews, and I have to stop the car.

I want to help him. I want to hold him and tell him that everything will be all right. At a red traffic light, I cautiously reach out to touch his knee, but he moves his leg away, not even looking at me after two hours on the road.

The stillness between us hurts like ten thousand needles penetrating my skin.

When we arrive in Mayfair, and it's only three more minutes to his home, I draw in a shaky breath and just say, "Please..."

A muscle jumps in his jaw, but Raffael doesn't reply. And then we arrive. The apartment building looms like a mountain of damnation before us. I park at the curb and turn off the engine, in hopes that—

No. Raffael grabs his backpack from the back seat and reaches for the door. In a panic I've never felt before in my life, I catch his arm and hold him back. It's more forceful than intended, so I ease my grip immediately when he leans back in the seat and frowns at my hand.

"Can I see you again...?" I croak because I don't know what else to say.

A long, silent moment passes. Then he begins to slowly shake his head. Before he can even finish, I blurt, full of fear, "Why not?"

"Because you— That kind of life isn't for me. It's *your* world. *Your* Wonderland. Not mine."

"Why do you say that? Because an old shrew couldn't keep her mouth shut?"

"No." For the first time since we left Eastbourne, Raffael lifts his gaze to meet mine. His lips are white like the rest of his face, only his eyes glisten with deep anguish. In a barely audible voice, he whispers, "Because people get burned for it."

I don't want to take my hand away from him. Can't. "Yes. By creatures that you can hardly call human," I reason.

"It doesn't matter. It happens. I don't want to be part of that world."

Shit, the calmer Raffael gets, the more the acute panic that I'm going to lose him engulfs me. "Then what will you do now?" My heart beats like the clopping hooves of a racehorse. "Pretend you like women? Get in a relationship? Get married and bend yourself all your life?"

"I don't need to be with anyone." His flat voice sends shivers down my spine as he removes my hand from his arm. "I can stay alone. Many people live like that."

No, no, no! Don't go! Don't do this to me. Please!

My fingers cramp around thin air. I can't swallow past the lump in my throat at the thought of leaving here in a minute—without him.

"Raffael..."

He opens the door.

No kiss, no touch, no nothing.

Just a look that says, "*Goodbye.*"

Forever...

And then, he's gone.

With a hard thud, the door slams shut on any possibility of a future together.

My heart stops beating with a pain I've never known before.

Raffael and I...was like catching a fragile snowflake in your hand, and in the next moment, it's already started to melt. There's nothing you can do to save it. In the end, you only see that drop of water on your palm where the snowflake once was. And it hurts.

God, it hurts so bad...

To be continued...

Awaking
TRUST
ANNA KATMORE

AWAKING TRUST

Sebastian came into my life in small, intense doses. Until I was addicted.

Now, breaking that addiction hurts worse than anything I've ever gone through before. I no longer know who I am, who I was, or even who I want to be. My world is shattered like the shards of my broken mirror. And seeing a bit of myself in all of those pieces, I know I'll never be whole again. Not without him.

Raffael doesn't believe in change. In possibilities. In us.

My heart bleeds as I walk away, even though it was necessary. But sometimes all it takes is one glance over your shoulder to realize that you can't stop fighting just yet. That maybe the battle is worth it. It's when you see the love of your life looking after you…breathless.

More books by Anna Katmore

ON THIN ICE
Counting Fireflies
Splintered North

*

Seventeen Butterflies

GROVER BEACH PLAYERS
Play With Me
Ryan Hunter
T Is For...
Dating Trouble
The Trouble with Dating Sue

FALL FOR ME
The Impossible Bet
Taming Chloe Summers

CRUSHED HEARTS
Unfair Love
Broken Dawn
Awaking Trust

ADVENTURES IN NEVERLAND
Neverland
Pan's Revenge

THE TRUE CHRONICLES OF FAIRYLAND
A Prince for Little Red Riding Hood
A Wolf in her Way

*

Eloyn
You were my Fairytale
My Secret Vampire
Three Shades of Sinful

About the author

At six years old, Anna Katmore told everyone she wanted to be an author after she discovered her mother's typewriter on a rainy afternoon. She could just see herself typing away on that magical thing for the rest of her life.

In 2012, she finished her first young adult romance "Play With Me" which was the beginning of her true writing career, with many books to follow.

Today, she lives in an enchanted world of her own, where she combines storytelling with teaching, and she never tires of bringing a little bit of magic into the lives of her beloved readers, too.

Anna's favorite quote and something she lives by:
If your dreams don't scare you, they aren't big enough.

For more information, please visit:
www.annakatmore.com

www.ingramcontent.com/pod-product-compliance
Lightning Source LLC
Chambersburg PA
CBHW060533160726
47991CB00001B/310